New York Times bestselling author M A Comley
Published by M A Comley
Copyright © 2015 M A Comley
Digital Edition, License Notes

This ebook is licensed for your personal enjoyment only. This ebook may not be re-sold or given away to other people. If you would like to share this book with another person, please purchase an additional copy for each recipient. If you're reading this book and did not purchase it, or it was not purchased for your use only, then please return to the site and purchase your own copy. Thank you for respecting the hard work of this author.

This is a work of fiction. Names, characters, places and incidents are a product of the author's imagination or are used fictitiously, and any resemblance to actual persons living or dead, business establishments, events or locales is entirely coincidental.

ISBN-13:978-1516866335

ISBN-10:1516866339

OTHER BOOKS BY
M A COMLEY
Blind Justice
Cruel Justice
Impeding Justice
Final Justice
Foul Justice
Guaranteed Justice
Ultimate Justice
Virtual Justice
Hostile Justice
Tortured Justice
Rough Justice
Dubious Justice
Forever Watching You
Wrong Place (DI Sally Parker thriller)
No Hiding Place (DI Sally Parker thriller) coming October 2015
Evil In Disguise – Based on True events novel.
Deadly Act (Hero series novella) coming Feb 2015
Torn Apart (Hero Series #1)
End Result (Hero Series #2)
Sole Intention (Intention Series #1)
Grave Intention (Intention Series #2)
Wrong Place (A DI Sally Parker thriller)
Merry Widow (A Lorne Simpkins short story)
It's A Dog's Life (A Lorne Simpkins short story)
A Time To Heal (A Sweet Romance)
A Time For Change (A Sweet Romance)
High Spirits
The Temptation Series (Romantic Suspense/New Adult Novellas)
Past Temptation (available now)
Lost Temptation (available now)
Keep in touch with the author at
http://www.facebook.com/pages/Mel-Comley/264745836884860
http://melcomley.blogspot.com
http://melcomleyromances.blogspot.com
Subscribe to newsletter

Calculated Justice

M A Comley

Prologue

The freshly cut grass silenced the man's footsteps. From behind the large blossoming shrub, he observed the woman inside the house, playing with her child. Crouched and ready to pounce, he glanced up at the sky as the darkening clouds sucked the light from the area. *Damn! It's going to piss down soon.* His pulse quickened when he realised that the woman had noticed the impending change in the weather, too. Fearing she was about to close the bi-fold doors to the kitchen, he scanned the area behind the prickly bush, searching for a clear path he could take to the house without alerting the woman to his presence.

The blonde woman gathered the child's toys from the patio and rushed back into the kitchen just as the heavens opened. Bypassing his original plan, he bolted for the door while her back was turned and she was preoccupied with her child. He grabbed her from behind and placed his hand over her mouth, muffling her screams. He leaned forward and twisted her head so she was looking at him. "Be quiet, and I promise not to hurt the kid. Scream, and I'll snap its fragile neck, then I'll do the same to you. You hear me?"

Tears quickly filled her wide eyes, and she nodded.

He released his hand and moved to stand alongside the child sitting in the highchair next to the table.

Her shaking hands entwined and clutched at her chest. "Please, please don't hurt us. If it's money you're after, I don't keep any in the house."

"It's not. It's *you* I'm after. You and the kid," he replied, revelling in the fear he'd struck in the woman.

"I... I don't understand."

"You will. Now, you, me, and the sprog, are going to take a nice ride in your car. I'll carry the kid just in case you get any idea of causing a scene outside."

She gasped. "I won't. I promise. Please don't hurt him. He's all I have."

The man looked around and laughed. "Really? You live in a mansion the size of ten football pitches, and you have the gall to say that?"

"Material things don't matter to me. All I care about is our safety, Jackson's safety."

He snorted. "What type of frigging name is that for a kid? He'll detest being teased at school for you lumbering him with that."

The woman fell silent. She looked confused but said nothing.

Good, at least she knows her place. I'm going to have fun with her.

She turned and looked over her shoulder towards the manicured garden.

"Don't even think about running, lady."

Shocked, she jerked her head around to face him. "I wasn't, I swear. I was going to close the door before we left."

He laughed wildly. "Want to secure the place, do you? What? To prevent anything untoward happening? I think it's too late for that, love."

"No... I mean, yes," her voice faltered.

"Right, I'll tell you what we're going to do. We're going to go upstairs and pack a bag—see how considerate I am?"

She nodded, her gaze flicking between him and her child.

"It's for my benefit. Don't relish living with the smell of your kid's dirty nappies filling the hideout for the next few days."

"Few days?"

"You have ten minutes, no more, to get a bag packed for the kid. You might want to chuck a change of clothes in for yourself, too. Nothing fancy, you won't need it where you're going." He laughed again.

The woman shuddered, closing her eyes in despair as he mocked her.

You ain't seen nothing yet, love. Just you wait and see what I've got lined up for you. "Is he still on the breast?"

"Sorry?"

He tutted. "You're not stupid. Is he still getting milk from your tits, bitch, or is he on formula milk by now?"

"No, from me. I'm feeding him."

He contemplated her answer and thought about where he intended keeping her once they arrived at their destination. "Well, that's going to have to change."

She gasped and fresh tears welled up in her eyes. "Please, don't. Jackson needs his mother's milk."

"Jackson gets what *I* tell him to have. You got that?"

"Yes. I don't want to argue—"

"Then don't. Any more crap like that, and I'll end the kid's life here and now. Am I making myself clear?"

"Yes, I'm sorry. The thing is, I don't have any formula in the house. We'll have to stop off and buy some."

Quick as a flash, he took a step forward, encroaching into her personal space, and snarled, "Let's get one thing straight from the outset, lady. *I* give the fucking orders, all right?"

Her breath caught on a sob. "Yes... I'm sorry. Forgive me." She wiped away the tears trickling in a steady flow from her eyes. He could tell she was trying but failing to remain strong.

He stepped away again. "You're forgiven, for now. Get a move on. You've got eight minutes and counting to get yourself sorted."

Hesitating, she waited for him to nod his approval before she ran from the room with him close behind her. The woman entered the second door on the right at the top of the stairs. She dithered, appeared to be in a flap, and almost barged into him as he stood in the doorway. "Slow down. What do you want?"

"An overnight bag from the main bedroom."

He stood aside, and she squeezed past him, her breasts brushing against his broad chest as she moved into the hallway. Her cheeks flushed. He stifled a laugh as his groin reacted to the incident. *Oh, yes, you're definitely going to have fun with her, boy!* He followed her into the walk-in dressing room just in case it turned out to be some kind of panic room; he never could tell with rich folks, not that he'd ever done such a thing before.

She tried to reach the bag on the top shelf but was too short. He tutted and grudgingly yanked the bag off the shelf, letting it drop to the floor with a thud. She paused for a second, and he tapped his watch, which prompted her to retrieve the bag and start sifting through her underwear drawer. She looked his way. "How many days?"

He hunched his shoulders up until they reached his ears. "One, two, ten. It all depends on how valuable you are to your hubby. Does he love you, Bethany Hardy?"

"Of course he does."

His shoulders dropped again. "Then maybe just pack for a day or two." He smiled and winked at her.

She continued to throw undies, T-shirts, and jeans into the bag. "The idea was to pack enough nappies and change of clothing for the kid, not *you*, but then that sums you women up nicely, doesn't it? Selfish to the core. We'll test that selfishness over the coming days. I can assure you of that."

"I'm not. I care for my child. I always put him first."

He held up his hand. "Get on with it, woman. Your acts have refuted your words already."

Bethany tipped the bag's contents onto the floor and stomped out of the room and down the hallway into the nursery, where she filled the bag with her child's things. With the bag full to bursting, she held it in both hands in front of her. "I'm done."

He chuckled inside. "What, nothing for you?"

"No. My baby comes first, every time."

He swallowed a nasty retort and pushed the woman ahead of him as they made their way down the sweeping curved staircase and back into the kitchen, where the child had started to cry. She threw the bag on the floor and rushed to comfort him.

"We haven't got time for that. Grab the kid, and let's go."

Bethany lifted the crying child from the highchair, smoothed back his hair, and kissed both his cheeks.

He picked up the bag she'd just packed and held out his hand. "The keys to your car?"

"They're hanging up over there."

"Right, we've wasted too much time already. Stick the kid in the car seat, and then I want you to drive. Be natural when you leave the house. React normally to the neighbours if you see any, and no one will get hurt. You do anything to raise their suspicions, and you have my word that the kid will get hurt, a life-changing injury. You have my word on that, okay?"

"I'll do as you say, I promise. There's no need to hurt us."

"Make sure you remain compliant, too, or else…" he warned as they left the house.

He put the woman's bag in the rear of the fancy Mercedes sports car and stood next to her as she strapped in the child, who had, thankfully, stopped crying. "Okay, get in. Put a smile on your face as we drive away."

"Where are we going?"

"Less questions. I'll give you the directions once we're out of here."

As they fastened their seatbelts, the old lady in a grand house opposite appeared on her doorstep and looked up and down the road before her eyes settled on them. He hid his face behind his hand when they drove past her gate. Bethany smiled and waved at the woman. He jabbed her in the thigh with his fist. "Just drive."

"Where to?"

Once they were out of sight of the old woman, he dropped his hand and pointed for her to turn right at the bottom of the road. "Get onto the motorway. Head towards Brighton."

"I have a satnav if it helps."

"It doesn't. And that's the last time you treat me like a fucking idiot. Got that?"

"I was just saying if you don't know the area, it will help us find the easiest route."

"Yeah, and the software is traceable by the police, too." His words caused a certain amount of panic to rise up within him. *You are a bloody idiot. You can't take her car. It's probably got a tracker installed.* His eyes darted the length of the street, which was relatively quiet for this time of day. Up ahead, a woman was getting out of another car. "Pull up behind that car," he ordered.

Confused, she glanced his way. "Why?"

He inhaled a deep breath. "Do it!" He slapped the dashboard, making her jump. The child started to cry in the back again. "Jesus Christ, doesn't it ever shut the fuck up?"

"Yes, but *he's* scared. We both are."

"Pull up, *now*. Turn off the engine and give me the keys." Once Bethany had handed him the keys, he left the vehicle and approached the woman. Her smile disappeared as he strode towards her. Her mouth opened, but his fist silenced her scream. She dropped to the ground. He dragged her onto the pavement then beckoned urgently for Bethany to join him. He snatched the keys from the woman's hand and pressed the key fob to open the Orion's doors. "Get in. I'll get the kid and the bag."

"We'll need his car seat, too."

"We don't have time. I'll hold him."

"You can't do that," she screeched.

His glare warned her to keep quiet. She climbed into the driver's seat. He retrieved the bag from the back and removed the child from the car seat. Then he dumped the bag in the Orion's boot and hopped in the passenger seat. She looked at him aghast.

"Don't even say it," he warned.

She closed her eyes as if in prayer then started the car and pulled away from the scene.

He glanced over his shoulder. *Sloppy, boy. Very sloppy. Not what I intended at all.*

CHAPTER ONE

Lorne managed to throw a quick cup of coffee and a slice of toast down her throat before she set off for the station. She felt exhausted after the unexpected exploits that had disrupted her weekend. When Tony asked for her help with a simple erection project in the paddock, she'd jumped at the chance to get her hands dirty once again, but neither of them had anticipated that the garden shed would take the whole weekend to put up. The weather had done everything it could to hamper their efforts, and by the time Sunday evening arrived, they both resembled waterlogged scarecrows and ached in every muscle imaginable. It was then that she'd reminded herself she was getting too old for such jobs. While the presence of mind and enthusiasm were still there in full strength, her ability to carry out such chores was dwindling rapidly. Lorne was approaching her forty-fifth birthday, but after the punishing weekend, she felt more like a woman on the verge of retirement.

Katy was getting out of her car when Lorne pulled into the car park at the station. She noted the green tinge to Katy's complexion, and her heart went out to her partner.

"Are you all right? Not morning sickness again?" Lorne asked, rushing to help steady her friend.

Katy leaned against the car and inhaled a few large breaths. "I'm not sure how long I can cope with feeling this shit all the time, Lorne. When does it wear off? Any idea?"

"Sorry, sweetie, that's like asking me how long the Forth Bridge is going to take to paint; everyone's experience is different. Why don't you ask Sean for some time off? You've been pushing yourself too hard lately. That's not good for either you or the baby."

"I hate to give in, but I fear you're right. The lethargy is overwhelming me. If I feel like this now, how the hell am I going to cope once the baby arrives?"

"I thought AJ and you had agreed that he was the one who was going to take care of the child. Has that changed?"

"No, we're still working along those lines. But I'll still be expected to do my share, won't I? I'm seriously having doubts about whether I'm cut out to be a mother at all."

Lorne placed both hands on Katy's arms. "Now you listen to me, young lady. You're going to be a superb mother. Things may look a little grim right now, but that'll change once you've held the little one in your arms—that much I can guarantee."

Katy sighed heavily. "I'll have to take your word on that. I think I'll call by and see Sean, all the same. That is if we haven't got a new case to deal with first thing."

"Even if we have, I can gather all the info on it while you sort things out with Sean."

"Deal. Hey, you're not looking your usual bright self, either. Are you okay?"

"Yeah, nothing a few cups of coffee won't put right."

"Ugh… I'm off the stuff at the moment. Doc's advice, plus I heave at the smell of roasted coffee beans."

"I think I was the same when I carried Charlie," Lorne said.

Lorne wished Katy luck then stepped into the incident room while her partner went on her mission to see the chief inspector.

AJ glanced up when she walked in. "Katy's here, looking peaky, though. She's gone to have a word with Sean. How is she at home?"

"Fidgety. She's struggling to keep food down most of the time. I'm concerned about both of them. Is this natural, Lorne? Do you think I should whisk her off to the doctor? Every time I suggest it, she snaps my head off."

Lorne rubbed his arm. "Bear with her, love. Her body is going through all sorts of changes right now. She loves you. Just keep telling yourself that."

He still looked down in the mouth, no matter what comfort he found in her words. "I'll be glad when the nine months gestation period is up, never mind how Katy feels."

Lorne laughed at the words he'd used, as if he were referring to a wild animal. "It'll be worth it in the end. Right, I'll just grab a coffee. Can I get you one?"

"That'll be great, thanks."

Lorne returned, carrying two cups of coffee. She handed AJ his cup and asked, "Any new cases come in?"

"Surprisingly, no. Very quiet weekend."

"Ugh… I know what that means. Prepare ourselves to be inundated later on."

The door to the incident room opened, and Lorne was perturbed to see a thunderous-looking Sean accompanying Katy into the room.

"Lorne, in my office if you will, immediately," he ordered sternly and left the room.

Katy avoided eye contact with Lorne as she rushed after her boss. Lorne swallowed nervously as she trotted along the hallway to his office. Sean's secretary smiled when she walked into the room. Lorne mouthed, "Is he all right?"

The secretary shrugged then began tapping the keyboard on her computer.

Lorne felt a large knot tighten her insides. *Shit! What have I done wrong now?*

Sean Roberts strode purposefully across his office and threw himself in his chair. She quietly closed the door behind her then tentatively joined him at his desk, waiting to be asked to take a seat.

"Well? Don't stand on ceremony for me, Lorne. Park your rear."

She half-smiled at him, sat down, and placed her hands in her lap like a nervous schoolgirl. "Good weekend, sir?"

"Yes. I haven't asked you in here to exchange pleasantries, Sergeant," he admonished swiftly.

"Sorry."

"There's no need." He let out a sigh and said, "What are we going to do with you?"

She frowned until her forehead began to ache. "What have I done wrong?" She wracked her tired brain and couldn't figure out what he was referring to. She hadn't stepped out of line in months, not to her knowledge anyway.

His face cracked into a smile. "I love winding you up. It gets easier as you get older."

Her hand covered her chest in relief. "You're sick. Has anyone ever told you that?"

"Plenty of times." He chuckled. "Right, back to business now my fun is over. As you're aware, Katy isn't feeling in the best of health at present. While I'm sympathetic to her condition, I do have a department to run and—"

Lorne gasped. "You're not going to sack her?"

"If you'll let me finish. No, I'm not *sacking* her—"

"You're demoting her then?"

He heaved another frustrated sigh, raised an eyebrow, and reclined in his chair. "Why don't you have a conversation with yourself? That might satisfy your need to establish the facts."

Lorne opened then shut her mouth and pretended to zip her lips.

"As I was saying, Katy isn't doing too well at the moment and wanted my advice on how to proceed with her pregnancy and working full time. The last thing I want is to lose her, so we've come to an agreement that she will stand down from her role as inspector and become a sergeant again."

Lorne's eyes almost fell onto the desk. "Crap, does that mean an outsider will be joining the team? You made this decision just this morning?" she asked in disbelief.

"No, I don't have anyone else in mind. I was hoping to persuade *you* to take on the role, permanently if need be. Also, no, Katy and I have discussed the issue several times over the past few weeks."

"Whoa… and none of you thought to tell me about this? I don't know whether to feel surprised or hurt by your admission, Sean."

"That's not really answering my question, Lorne, is it? Will you become the team's Inspector again?"

She crossed her arms and chewed her lip before she answered. "You know I have to run this past Tony before I accept the position. This has come as a bombshell, sir, totally unexpected to me."

"I understand your need to discuss this with Tony. What do you think he'll say?"

She blew out a breath that puffed out her cheeks. "Hard to tell. I think he'll be thrilled and hesitant at the same time. His business is still in its infancy but doing well at the moment. I'd like to be around to give him a hand with that and running the home and kennel, although Charlie is doing a fab job there, too…"

"Sounds to me you're searching for a reason to back out of the promotion on offer, Sergeant."

"No, not in the slightest, merely stating facts. We made a pact when we got married. Although, I must admit I did enjoy filling in for Katy a few months back when her dad was ill."

"So? When can I expect a definitive answer? Tomorrow?"

"Jeez… no pressure on your part, of course. As a matter of interest, what would happen if I turned you down?"

He shrugged. "The post has to be filled. If you decline, then I'll have a surplus of sergeants on the team, and one of you will have to be transferred to another department. On the other hand, this scenario makes perfect sense. All it means is that you and Katy will be swapping roles."

"Okay. Can you give me twenty-four hours?"

"Of course. I'm sure Tony will be the first to congratulate you on your new role as inspector."

"Yes, you're probably right. I just don't feel comfortable about going back on my word to him. That's all. What about Katy? If she's feeling rough—I hate to say it—but won't that affect her ability to work full time? A sergeant's role isn't really any easier than an inspector's, is it?"

"I agree. The team are great at covering each other's backs, though. If she needs to take it easy now and again, I'm sure AJ or Karen will be willing to fill her shoes and accompany you when you need to go out and about. Mind you, after that last case we cracked together, I might even be tempted to tag along for the odd ride, too."

"Christ, if ever there was an incentive for me to turn down the promotion, you just did a fab job at presenting it." She grinned.

"Cheeky mare. I must get on. Let me know first thing either way tomorrow, okay?"

Lorne stood and walked towards the door. "You've got it."

When Lorne returned to the incident room, Katy had obviously filled the rest of the team in on the meeting she'd had with Roberts. They were all looking at her expectantly, awaiting her announcement. "Don't look at me like that, you lot. I have to chat about this with Tony first."

Katy marched into her office and threw over her shoulder, "That's a yes then. Drinks are on Lorne after work."

"Now wait just a minute. I haven't agreed, and I certainly won't be in Tony's good books if I turn up late tonight," she objected. But the thrill of being an inspector again sent an unexpected shiver down her spine. She shook her head and sat down at her sergeant's desk. Every now and again, she glanced over at her old office and savoured the memories it evoked. She smiled as Pete's face appeared in her mind. He was nodding, giving her the go-ahead to accept the challenge. She'd been fortunate enough to have worked alongside two great partners over the years. She hoped Katy could hang in there and not give in to being a full-time mum. *Does this mean I've already accepted the role?* She knew she had. She was confident that Tony would back her decision one hundred percent, too. She knew he would call her a numpty for not accepting the role on the spot, but there was a method to Lorne's madness—she needed to keep her boss on his toes from the word go to prevent him from taking her for granted again. Although, to be fair, that had taken place under the leadership of their previous superintendent. Lorne refused to go back to those days, and she couldn't really see the same turmoil being thrown at her while Anne White, the new super, was in charge. She liked and admired the woman, who seemed to reciprocate Lorne's feelings.

The morning dragged by as Lorne tied up loose ends to several small cases the team had successfully concluded in the last few weeks. Nothing major had needed their attention for over a week, which had given them a much-needed breather.

Lorne looked up from her computer screen and watched Katy make yet another trip to the loo. Her heart sank when Katy returned, pale-faced and with damp hair. Lorne didn't envy her partner in the least.

Just before lunch, Lorne insisted they should get some fresh air and go to the local park to eat their sandwiches for a change. However, that idea flew out the window when AJ answered a call at his desk and signalled that it was a significant call.

Lorne waited anxiously until he hung up. "What is it? Sounded bloody serious, AJ."

"That was a friend of a friend who thought I should know about an incident that he'd heard about."

"Get to the point, AJ!" Katy snapped. "Sorry. Go on."

AJ looked down at his notes. "Well, it would appear that the wife and son of a very wealthy businessman have gone missing."

Lorne and Katy glanced at each other and frowned before Katy replied, "What does that have to do with us? We're not a missing persons team. We're a murder squad."

"I know. This guy owes me a few favours; he said that something doesn't feel right concerning the case and thought he would bring it to my attention."

"A few favours, eh?" Lorne queried. She turned to Katy. "No harm in checking it out, I guess. It's not as if we're inundated with cases right now."

Katy snorted and shook her head. Her eyes glinted when she said, "You speak for yourself. My desk is in fear of collapsing under the strain of the amount of shitty paperwork piled on it. Still, that won't be my problem after today. I'm willing to leave that for the new DI to deal with when *she* takes over tomorrow."

"Huh! Well, that aside, I'm thinking we should check this out."

"Then I'm willing to go with your intuition on this one. What's the address, AJ?"

He handed Katy the slip of paper, then Lorne and Katy collected their jackets and left the station. During the short drive into the heart of London, Katy rubbed her tummy. "I think you should take the lead on this one."

"Still feeling icky? I don't mind."

"Yeah. Thanks, partner," Katy replied, smiling gratefully.

They took the lift up to Mr. Lance Hardy's penthouse office, where Lorne showed the young redhead sitting at the tempered-glass desk her warrant card, and asked to speak to Mr. Hardy. The PA seemed surprised to see them and walked into the office behind her. She returned a few moments later and instructed Lorne and Katy to follow her.

Lance Hardy looked up from his paperwork and motioned for them to take a seat. Lorne guessed the man was in his mid-to-late thirties; he had strikingly handsome features, and the cut of his suit screamed that he was a very wealthy man. His surroundings, a penthouse office overlooking the financial quarter of London, also emphasised his status. "How can I help you?" he asked, somewhat offhand.

Lorne looked him straight in the eye. "We hear that your wife and child have gone missing."

He seemed agitated by the news and slammed his gold pen on the desk. "Who told you?"

"Does it matter?"

"Yes. I thought if I came running to the police, it would put my family in further jeopardy."

"I see. So how were you going to deal with the situation alone? Furthermore, how is it possible for you to deal with their disappearance while sitting behind your desk, Mr. Hardy?" Lorne knew she sounded harsh, but to her, the man's actions and demeanour made no sense at all.

"Because, if I don't go about my daily business, Sergeant, my wife will have nothing left to come home to."

"Really? You're putting materialistic things before your family's well-being?"

"No, that's not what I said. In my line of business, if I take a single day off, I could lose millions. In the current economic climate, that option really isn't available to me at present."

Lorne's pulse raced. *Is this guy for real? I've met some pretty heartless men over the years, but he's got to be the top of the pile.*

"Okay, in that case, you're guilty of putting your *business* before your family's needs. I apologise for not comprehending that in the first instance."

He fell back against his plush, leather-padded chair and ran a hand through his short brown hair. "I'm sorry if that's how it came across to you, Sergeant. It wasn't my intention. What I'm trying to say is, I fear my wife and son have been kidnapped, and I suppose I've been in a quandary ever since. Should I go to the police or not? If I do, would the kidnapper end their lives? I'm sure you've encountered this kind of stalemate before numerous times."

Lorne could tell he was just trying to justify his workaholic behaviour. "Actually, no."

His mouth twisted. "Then I'm sorry if I'm coming across as being a heartless bastard. I love my wife and child. Every waking moment, I think of them. Every damn hour I spend in this office, over a hundred hours a week, is so their lives are the best they can possibly be."

"Really? And how does your wife feel about that level of neglect, Mr. Hardy?"

"Neglect? Are you *crazy*? Have you not listened to a word I've said? Everything I do is for them."

Katy nudged her knee against Lorne's, and she took the hint to come at the man from a different angle. "How do you know your wife has been kidnapped? Couldn't she have just taken your child and left?"

He tutted and sighed heavily. "No! My wife loves me. I love my wife and son more than life itself—she knows that. Bethany would never just up and leave. Besides, all her clothes are still at the house. Would someone intent on walking out on their partner truly leave without packing a suitcase?"

"So, you're telling us that nothing is missing from your home at all?"

"No. I'm telling you that my wife and child are missing from my home."

"Apart from them?" Lorne asked impatiently.

"Now that you mention it, there was something suspicious I found in our bedroom."

Lorne's interest piqued. "Such as?"

"I found a pile of my wife's clothes on the floor in our dressing room. That struck me as odd."

"Is your wife usually house-proud? Is that what you're saying?"

"Yes, extremely."

"If no suitcases are missing, what about a vanity case, overnight bag, something like that?"

He shook his head. "I'm not sure. Not that I've noticed, but then Bethany takes care of that side of things."

"Anything missing from the nursery, perhaps?"

"I don't know."

"Why?" Lorne asked abruptly.

"I understand what you're getting at. Yes, it's because I'm always at work, Sergeant. As I've already stated, I work very long hours so my wife can remain at home, bringing up our son. Is that wrong in your eyes, Sergeant?"

"No. I find it admirable, if you must know. I still need to ask the question, though, Mr. Hardy. Why are you reluctant to report them missing?"

"May I ask how you know about their disappearance?" he retorted quickly.

Lorne contemplated her response carefully. "Your case came into our office this morning."

"And how is that possible? Have you asked yourself that, Sergeant?"

"I'm not sure what you're suggesting, Mr. Hardy. Care to elucidate?"

"In my own subtle way, I have been putting the word out about my family. It's difficult to come right out and ask the media for their help. I'm guessing there will be a ransom, because we're perceived to be wealthy, which is why I'm trying to do things discreetly. The last thing I want to do is put my family's life in more danger than it is already. I'm not that insensitive; please don't assume that I am."

"I see. That makes sense. So, how can we help going forward? Would you rather we ignore your case?"

He sat forward and buried his head in his hands. After a few seconds, his hands dropped onto the desk with a thud, and when he looked up at them, his blue eyes were sparkling with tears. "I don't know. I'm damned if I get you involved and damned if I don't. Look at how you've come here today and treated me. Not as a victim but as a suspect."

"I beg to differ. As an investigator, I'm obligated to try and establish the facts from the outset. If I've offended you in any way then I'm truly sorry about that. I repeat, how would you prefer to proceed with this investigation? If you agree to the help we're prepared to offer you, then we'll pull out all the stops to bring your family back home safely. If on the other hand, you decline our help, then we'll walk away immediately and let you deal with the consequences. Hopefully, you don't regret your decision when your family are reported dead."

"See! The options suck, either way."

"I'm not trying to make your dilemma an impossible one, believe me. But if you agree to our help, then we can set up tracing equipment on your phones in case the kidnapper gets in touch. However, I should add a word of caution here: once the police are involved in a case, certain kidnapping cases have gone awry. There truly are no guarantees."

He shrugged in resignation and held out his hands, placing one higher than the other and then alternating them. "Yes or no. It's a tough decision to make without taking the time to consider everything, Sergeant. Can you leave me to think things over? I'll give you a call later, before your shift ends, perhaps."

Lorne and Katy rose from their chairs, and Lorne handed him a business card. "Give me a call, day or night. I will urge you to make your decision promptly, though, Mr. Hardy. There's no telling how long we have before the person contacts you."

"I understand. I need to ring a few relatives, get their advice first."

"You do that. One last question, when did your family go missing?"

"Sometime yesterday, although I have no idea of the time."

"And they definitely went missing from your home? Is that correct?"

He shrugged and stood up. "As far as I know. I have nothing to corroborate my assumption."

"Okay. Thank you for your time. When we get back to the office, we'll have a scout around for any incidents that have been reported in the vicinity of your home."

"Thank you."

When she shook his hand, Lorne noted it felt clammy.

Back in the car, Katy asked, "What do you think?" Her hand moved gently over the slight bulge in her tummy.

"I'm inclined to believe him. I intentionally hit him hard to begin with just to see his reaction. We get so many cases where the husbands bump off the wife. I needed to be sure that wasn't what we're dealing with here."

"I'm not so sure. If he had nothing to do with their disappearance, why wouldn't he jump at the chance for us to get involved?"

"Like he said, it's not as clear cut as that, Katy. Are you all right?"

"No. I'm feeling nauseous again. I think I'll give lunch a miss, if that's all right."

"It's not. You have to eat. If you bring it up afterwards, fine. At least the little one will be getting some sustenance to help him or her grow. Think of the baby, eh?"

Katy exhaled noisily. "I do, *constantly*. It's bloody hard not to. All right, maybe a light salad or something along those lines."

"Great idea. Let's stop off at the pub, and I'll have a word, see what they can rustle up for you that won't make you want to reintroduce it to the world ten minutes later."

Katy grinned. "Going back to Hardy—you never asked if he had any enemies."

"I will. It's not our case yet. I didn't want to waste time asking if he wasn't going to accept my offer. Does that make sense?"

"Yep, perfect sense to me." Katy wound down the window and sucked in a mouthful of fresh air.

If only people understood the trauma the body goes through during pregnancy, I think more people would reject the idea of becoming pregnant altogether. Poor Katy!

CHAPTER TWO

Lorne was even more concerned about Katy after seeing the way she nibbled and messed around with her salad. She made a mental note to have a word with AJ once they got back to the station.

Katy gingerly climbed the stairs behind Lorne and turned right to go to the ladies' loo, while Lorne continued into the incident room. She rushed up to AJ's desk and spoke in a hushed voice, "Has Katy visited the doctor lately? I'm worried she's not consuming enough calories."

"Not for a couple of weeks." He raised his hands and sat back in his chair. "If I mention anything about food, she gives me a death stare—that is, if she's not snapping my head off. I'm at a loss as to what to say or what to do for the best."

"Well, her first priority should be the baby."

Katy entered the room and glanced at them through narrowed eyes. "Telling tales on me, Sergeant?"

"Was I?" she asked AJ, winking at him.

"Nope. You look pale. Have you been sick again?" AJ asked with a concerned smile.

Katy glared at her fella. "Don't start. Anything of note happen while we've been out?"

"Actually, Karen had a call of interest. She can give you the details."

Lorne and Katy moved around the room to see Karen, who was awaiting their arrival with her notepad in hand. "I finished the files I was working on, and took the liberty of searching the recent calls that have been logged, to see if anything cropped up around the area of the Hardys' home. I figured that would be your next stop once you'd visited Mr. Hardy. I hope I did the right thing?"

Lorne nodded. Karen had exceptional instincts and superb organisational skills, which often proved invaluable. "It depends if you found anything of interest."

"I did. Mr. Hardy probably told you that his wife's vehicle has already been found."

Lorne glanced at Katy and frowned. "No, he didn't. Where?"

"How strange," Karen replied then continued, "In Castlebury Road, a few feet away from their home."

"Is this some kind of joke? Why in God's name wouldn't he divulge that?" Katy asked, her bemusement matching Lorne's.

"The plot thickens. What else can you tell us, Karen?" Lorne asked.

"Well, the reason this came to light was because one of the Hardys' neighbours was attacked by a man who went on to steal her car."

"So, she reported the incident, I take it. Did she mention if Mrs. Hardy was with the man or not?"

"I don't know, boss. Do you want me to give the woman a call?"

Lorne shook her head. "No. I think we should pay her a visit in person. Anything else?"

"No. I haven't had a chance to run the licence number yet, to see if any other incidents have occurred with the stolen vehicle since."

"Okay, do that and give me a ring on my mobile if you find anything." Lorne turned to Katy. "Are you up for another trip out?"

Katy nodded. "Even if I wasn't, you couldn't stop me from coming with you."

After thirty minutes of battling heavy traffic, they pulled up outside the victim's house.

"Let's hope she's in," Katy said.

"After we've had a word with the woman, I think we should take a look around the Hardys' home."

"What? Inside?" Katy looked stunned.

"No. Outside. I have a feeling Mr. Hardy will call back later and give us the go-ahead to investigate. Having a quick shufty around the property now will save us time, agreed?"

Katy hitched her right shoulder. "You're going to do it anyway, even if I try and tell you not to."

Lorne sniggered. "That I am. Let's go."

A woman sporting a painful-looking swollen split lip answered the door, opening it only a few inches.

Lorne thrust her warrant card through the crack. "Hello, Mrs. Jenkins. I'm DS Lorne Warner, and this is my partner, DI Katy Foster. I hope it's convenient for us to have a chat about the incident you reported the other day."

She hesitated then finally allowed them to enter her home. Lorne and Katy walked through the hallway into the huge kitchen-cum-sunroom at the rear of the property.

"I was just about to have a coffee. Would you like one?"

Lorne nodded. "That would be lovely. Thank you."

"Sorry, can I have a cup of tea instead?" Katy asked.

While the woman made the drinks, Lorne asked, "How have you coped since the incident?"

"To be honest, my nerves are shattered. That's the first time I've opened the front door to anyone. If you had been men, I don't think I would have bothered."

"Sorry to hear that. It must have been a shock for you. Do you feel up to telling us about it?"

Mrs. Jenkins put the china mugs on a tray and led Lorne and Katy across the room to the table, situated in front of wooden French doors that overlooked the beautifully tended back garden. She pulled in a large breath and stared at her hands, clasping her mug. "All I did was nip out to the shops to pick up a few bits and pieces—and bam... the man walked up to me and hit me."

"No conversation at all?"

"Nothing. Had he asked for my keys, I would have handed them over... I think, rather than end up with a thick lip and a couple of wobbly teeth. There's too much bloody violence in this world."

"I agree; there is. Did you see anyone with him? What direction he came from perhaps?"

"No. I unloaded my car, locked it, turned round, and before I could ask what he wanted, he thumped me. I was knocked unconscious, according to Marj, the woman who came to my rescue."

"Did Marj see the incident for herself?" Lorne asked.

"No. She found me lying on the pavement. I don't think I was out for long before she came along."

"Was anything taken at the time, such as your handbag?"

"No. Just my car. Have there been other crimes similar to this reported in this area? Is that why you're here?"

"Not exactly. We do think the incident is linked to another crime that was committed at the same time. Unfortunately, we can't really go into detail on that."

"Really? In the same road? How odd. I haven't heard anything about that."

"It's not common knowledge at the moment. A very sensitive case, shall we say."

"I see, I think."

"I know it's probably a long shot, but do you think you would be able to identify the man if you saw him again?"

"In a line-up? That kind of thing?" Mrs. Jenkins asked.

"Either that—of course we'd have to catch the man first—or would you be willing to give a description to an artist?"

The woman closed her eyes for a second. "It all happened so fast. I'm just trying to see if I can conjure up enough details for you. To be honest, I'm not sure I can supply you with much."

"A rough sketch is sometimes all we need. Most people, once they get started, end up remembering far more than they ever imagined they could."

"Okay, I'm willing to at least try. I'd like nothing better than to see him put away. Is there any news on my car yet?"

"No. We've put out an alert on the vehicle. Once you've worked with the sketch artist, I can call a press conference, get all the media involved. We'll mention your car during that in the hope that someone recognises it."

"Thank you. It might not have been much, but I'm lost without the car. It's my lifeline to the outside world since my husband passed away."

"I'm sorry to hear that, Mrs. Jenkins. Hasn't the insurance company supplied you with a replacement car?"

"To be honest, I haven't even contacted them." She held her trembling hand out in front of her. "I'm still so shaken up by the assault that I'm having trouble thinking straight at present. I'll get on to them this afternoon."

"I'm not sure they'll be much help, but you have the crime number. Give them that and let them sort out the details for you. So, when shall we organise the artist to come and see you?"

"Any time. You need the information promptly, don't you?" She took a sip of her drink.

"We do. I can arrange for someone to bring the artist to you this afternoon, rather than you dragging down the station, if that's okay with you?"

"That would be wonderful. Not sure I'm up to venturing out just yet."

"Is there anything else you can tell us? Have you noticed anyone in the road acting suspiciously lately?"

The woman remained silent then clicked her fingers and pointed at her. "There was a man. Last week. I had to take the cat to the vet's and noticed a man outside the Hardys' home."

Lorne raised an eyebrow. "What day? Can you remember?"

"On Monday of last week…" She paused, closed her eyes for a second, then gasped. "Do you know what? If my memory isn't playing tricks on me, I would swear it was the same man who hit me and stole my car."

"Are you sure about that?"

Her eyes flickered shut again. Moments later, they flew open. "Yes, I'm almost certain it's the same person." She gasped a second time. "Has something untoward occurred at the Hardys' home? Is that the incident you were referring to before?"

"Possibly. We really can't go into detail yet mainly because we don't know a great deal about it. Well, the sooner we get the artist to you, the quicker we can organise the media's input. Can you call the station, Katy?"

Katy nodded and left the table to make the call from the hallway. She returned within minutes. "The artist can be here at three this afternoon, if that's okay?"

Mrs. Jenkins nodded. "That suits me fine, dear."

"Well, thanks for the drink, Mrs. Jenkins. Please, try not to worry. I know it's difficult under the circumstances, but I think this incident was a one-off and you just happened to be in the wrong place at the wrong time. I'd hate to think of you walking around in constant fear because of this," Lorne said.

"I'm sure I will be fine once I hear you have caught the man responsible, Sergeant. Please, do your best."

"You have my word on that. Don't forget to ring the insurance company after we leave."

"I won't. Thank you. Good luck with your mission, ladies."

Lorne and Katy bade the woman farewell, jumped in the car, and drove the short distance to the Hardys' home. Getting out of the car, Lorne looked around then led Katy up the driveway to the mansion. "I think we should go around the back. Can you see any form of surveillance?"

"Nope. How ridiculous is that? And furthermore, why isn't there a bloody gate on the property? Surely someone in his position would be more up on personal security," Katy said.

"Maybe that's what his problem is—he feels guilty about not protecting his family more."

"You could be right. Can I ask what you're hoping to find, Lorne?"

"I have no idea. I really just wanted to try and figure out how the abductor gained access to the property. It's pretty obvious now that we're here. Let's see what we can find around the back of the house."

Lorne followed the concrete path to the side of the property. "This is too easy. What is wrong with these people?"

"It does seem odd. Perhaps they've only just moved in."

Reaching the back garden, Lorne waited for Katy to catch up with her. "I never thought of that. Remind me to put that to him later. Looking around, there's no real sign that this is a young person's garden. No swings or the obligatory trampoline. The patio is kind of small, too small for entertaining corporate people anyway. You could be on the money with your assumption, partner."

Katy nodded. Lorne ventured farther into the garden and peered through the large patio doors into the pristine black-and-white gloss kitchen. "That's strange."

"What is?" Katy asked, joining her.

"Not a plate or cup out of place, as if it hasn't been used."

"Well, Hardy did say that he spends a lot of time at the office. If his family isn't here, why would he want to come home?"

"Good point. On the other hand, wouldn't you want to be at home in case the kidnapper tried to make contact? What are we missing here?"

"Without him confiding in us, Lorne, I'm not sure we're ever going to find out."

"Let's get back to the station. I want to do a thorough check on our Mr. Hardy."

"I'd do the same if I was still in charge," Katy mumbled, referring to the imminent change in their relationship, as they wound their way back up the path to the front of the house, towards the car.

CHAPTER THREE

The man, who went by the nickname of Warrior, watched the woman breast-feeding her child, neglecting to give her the privacy she was obviously longing for. Her face flushed violently, making him chortle now and again. The sound of his mobile ringing tore him out of his fixated state.

"Yep," he answered.

"Where's the woman?" the caller demanded abruptly.

"Feeding the kid. Nice pair of tits she's got, by the way."

"Keep your hands off her. That's not part of the deal. You hear me?"

"I hear ya. I ain't touched her. Like I said, she's feeding the kid, as in breast-feeding it."

The caller tutted his annoyance. "I'm about to put the next part of the plan in place. Are you all set at your end?"

"Yep, I'll make the calls as instructed. First to him and then to the bitch herself. I'm going to enjoy making that second call. She won't know what's hit her."

"Go softly, softly at first, like I suggested. We want her to feel confused and out of her depth to begin with, before we up the game and see her really spin out of control. I'm going to enjoy seeing her being out of her depth—the bitch deserves all we've got lined up for her and more."

"I'll ring you when I've been in touch with both parties." Warrior pushed the End Call button. He went back to ogling the woman, his mind running through what lay ahead of him and his crew. "What are you looking at?" he snarled.

"Nothing. Please, whatever you're planning, my husband has the money to pay you off. Please, I'm begging you not to hurt me or my child."

"Yeah, yeah, beg all you like, love. I'll do what's necessary in order for us to achieve our goal."

"Which is what?" she asked.

He tapped the side of his nose. "That would be for me to know, lady, and you to find out, *eventually*. And I assure you, you *will* find out soon enough. Are you nearly done there? 'Cause I've got important work to do, and you need to go back in your 'little den.'" He laughed as her face froze in fear.

"Please, I'll behave. You don't have to put me in there again. I promise I won't try anything again."

"Too bloody right you won't. That'll teach you not to treat all men as idiots. Now finish up quickly. He's munched long enough on your tits as it is. I've got more important things to do, lady."

The woman glared at him. She stroked the child's head comfortingly and removed her breast from his mouth. After rearranging her blouse, she placed the child in the makeshift cot she had constructed out of the overnight bag she'd packed with the child's clothes. He'd admired her ingenuity for a split second when she'd thought up the idea to care for her child's needs. That was before he'd forced her into her hidey-hole for the first time. Reluctantly she stood and walked towards the back door of the old farmhouse. "I'm ready."

He opened the back door, grabbed her arm, and marched her over to the hole in the ground. He lifted the wooden door and prodded her in the back.

She crouched, placed her hands on either side of the hole, and eased herself into the wooden carcase. Once she was lying stretched out, there were barely two inches either side for her to move. "Please, let me be with my baby?"

He answered her by slamming the door shut then locked it with the huge metal key. He leaned down and grinned when he heard her begin to sob. Time was getting on. As much as he would have loved to stay there and listen to the woman's pitiful crying and praying, he had a schedule to keep.

When he returned to the house, he was relieved to see that the baby was fast asleep. "Thank Christ for that." He searched the drawer of the pine dresser in the small dining room to find the contact numbers his boss had given him. He dialled the first number — Hardy's office. "Hardy, I have your wife and child. If you do as I say, they won't get hurt."

"Crap. Please don't hurt them. I have money. How much do you need?"

"I'll come to that in a moment. *I'm* calling the shots. Shut up and listen. The money side of things will be covered once I've told you what I want."

"You mean this isn't about the money?"

"Shut up and listen," Warrior warned, his knuckles turning white as his anxiety heightened. He hated talking on the phone to strangers at the best of times. With the added task of not trying to give away any unnecessary details, his angst was in the severe overload realms already. He covered the phone, sucked in a large breath then released it. "You need to contact a certain copper. I'll give you her details in a moment. I need to have her on-board before I can take this any further. Got that?"

"Yes. Let me get a pen and paper. Okay, I'm ready."

Warrior read the name from the sheet of paper in his hand. "You've got to contact a Lorne Simpkins—or she could be going under the name of Warner, not sure which—of the Met Police."

"What? Let me check something."

Warrior heard rustling on the other end of the phone and tapped his foot in annoyance until the man came back on the line.

"Yes, I thought so. She was here today, in my office. What has this got to do with her?"

"Never you mind. All will become apparent soon enough. I want you to call her and work with her to try and solve the disappearance of your family."

"I don't understand. Why?"

"No questions. Just do as I say, or else…"

"Okay. Are my wife and son all right?"

"For the moment, yes."

The man sighed with relief.

"They'll remain unharmed, providing you do everything I ask. You hear me? Although, from now on, I will no longer be speaking with you direct. I'll be contacting Simpkins. Got that?"

"Then why do you want *me* to place the call instead of you making contact with the detective yourself?"

"You ask a lot of dumb questions, especially when you've been warned not to." Warrior moved towards the baby and kicked the bag softly. The baby woke up with a start and began crying.

"Please, don't hurt Jackson. I'm sorry. Tell me what to say or do, and I'll do it, to the letter."

"I thought you'd say that. The second I hang up, I want you to call Simpkins and ask her to take on your case. Then tell her to expect a call from me within the hour. Now do it! And, Hardy, any funny business, and you have my word your child will get hurt first and then your wife. Don't force my hand, okay?"

"I understand. I'll ring her now. Just, please show compassion when dealing with my family."

Warrior laughed then hung up. He paced the room for the next thirty minutes until he felt he'd given Hardy enough time to contact Simpkins and for her to be waiting apprehensively for him to ring her. Then he dialled the number and smiled when Lorne's mobile was answered immediately. "Ah, that was prompt. Glad to see that, Simpkins. Keep up the good work during the process that lies ahead of you, and you won't go wrong."

"Who are you?"

"My name is Warrior. That's all you need to know. Well, that and this snippet of information. You need to follow every inch of this plan to its conclusion—one slip up and the Hardys will be killed, all three of them."

"Okay, you've got my attention. First things first, I need something in return."

"You're not in any position to start bartering with me, lady."

"I appreciate that. All I'm asking is that you give me proof of life at regular intervals right up to the end."

"That's doable. How's this for starters?" He kicked the bag again to set the baby off. "One crying baby, okay?"

"Yes, please, don't hurt them. I'll do anything and everything you ask. You needn't worry on that score."

"You know what? I ain't worried in the slightest. You know something else, Madame Detective? *You* bloody well should be worried. I'm going to be generous and give you the day off. Make sure you use your time off wisely, because starting at seven a.m. tomorrow, you're going to be running around like your head has been chopped off, if you get my drift."

"Oh, I get your drift all right, Warrior. Let's hope I can achieve all that you want from me."

"Only time will tell. Until tomorrow, Sergeant."

"As of tomorrow, you can call me 'Inspector.'"

Noting the hint of defiance in her tone, he laughed then hung up. "I'm going to enjoy this battle, Simpkins. Not sure you're going to feel the same way after you see what I have in store for you."

CHAPTER FOUR

The instant Lorne ended the call with the kidnapper, she turned to Katy. "We should go and fill Sean in. We need to take this guy seriously from the kick-off."

"I agree."

They raced along the corridor. Outside Sean's office, his secretary greeted them with a puzzled look. "Inspector, Sergeant, I don't see a meeting scheduled in the chief's diary."

"It's urgent. Is he free?" Lorne asked.

"No. The super is in there with him."

"That's even better. We can tell them both at the same time. They'll want to see us, I promise."

The young woman rose from her seat and knocked on her boss's door. "Sorry to interrupt. I have Lorne and Katy here to see you. They insist it's urgent."

"Send them in."

The secretary pushed open the door for Lorne and Katy to walk into the room then closed the door behind them.

"What's the urgency?" Sean frowned as his gaze drifted between Lorne and Katy.

"I fear we have a grave situation on our hands. A kidnapping. We followed up on an innocent call about a woman's car being stolen this morning, and it's kind of escalated quickly from there."

"Take a seat and fill us in on the events," the chief instructed.

Lorne told her superiors about visiting Mr. Hardy and the fact he was undecided about getting the police involved in his wife and child's disappearance. "But now, the decision has been taken out of his hands because the kidnapper has made contact with us directly."

"Whom did he ring?" Sean asked, his eyes narrowing.

"Me," Lorne admitted.

Anne folded her arms and placed the forefinger and thumb of her right hand either side of her chin. "Why? What are you suggesting, Sean?" she asked.

"I just wondered. It seems a bit odd to contact Lorne when Katy is still the inspector on the team, until the changeover."

Lorne contemplated his reply for a split second. "That sounds kind of ominous. You think this is someone I know, Chief?"

"Sounds that way to me. How did he address you?"

Lorne quickly replayed the conversation in her mind. "To start with, he just called me Simpkins. My God! I didn't even think about that at the time."

Sean pointed at her. "That's what I wanted to know. So we're dealing with someone from a few years ago. How long have you been calling yourself Warner?"

"Tony and I will be celebrating our sixth anniversary this year."

"So, you need to go through all those you've had dealings with in the past and see what comes up."

Lorne's mouth hung open for an instant then slammed shut again. "Are you kidding me?"

"No. The sooner you get on with that, the quicker we'll work out who we're dealing with."

Lorne thought his suggestion over for a second. "Okay, supposing you're right, how does this connect to Hardy? I've never even met the man before today."

"Who says there has to be a connection to him?"

"He's right, Lorne," Katy piped up. "If the kidnapper's aim is to get to you, perhaps they just plucked Hardy's name out of a hat. The fact that he's mega rich is probably just a bonus in the kidnapper's eyes."

"Whoa, hold on a sec. You think this is wholly about me? Are you both insane?"

"Make that three of us, Lorne," the super added.

Lorne's mouth dried up, and her heart sank. "I need to tell my family immediately if that's the case. I hope to Christ you're all wrong about this. I can't go through this living hell again." Tears misted her eyes, and she swallowed the lump forming in her throat as one specific image filtered her mind. She tried her hardest to rid her mind of the vile image but failed.

Katy reached over and clasped her hand. "You know it can't be him, love."

Sean left his chair and sat on the desk in front of her. He reached for her other hand and squeezed it. "Katy's right. There's no way this could be connected to the Unicorn—you killed him, Lorne."

She smiled through her tears and sniffed. "Knowing that bastard, he'll do his best to make my life unbearable from his grave. Mark my words on that."

"Tell me what you need, Lorne? Protection for your family? You've got it," Sean said.

She shrugged. "How the hell do I know? We could be blowing this up out of all proportion. The fact that we're all thinking along the same lines must mean something, right?"

"Okay, let's back up here," Anne intervened. "I vaguely remember hearing about the case. Would someone care to refresh my memory of what occurred?"

Sean patted Lorne's hand, winked at her, and returned to his seat. "He was the mastermind behind a scandal that rocked London—what? About eight years ago now, Lorne?"

She nodded after doing a quick calculation in her head.

Sean continued, "If I remember rightly, it was how Lorne and Tony got together."

She winced, and the heat in her cheeks quickly returned. "Not exactly. That happened in France, when we hunted him down. That's beside the point anyway."

Sean winked at her again, as if apologising for causing her to be embarrassed. "He threatened all sorts, kidnapped Lorne's daughter, Charlie, and… well, he did a lot of things to the women he'd forced to be part of a human-trafficking ring, shall we say."

"Ah, yes, I remember now. The case made you reconsider your career in the force as I recall, Lorne. I do hope, if we find out there is a connection to this man, that you'll be stronger this time round. We need you. I'm not being selfish by taking Katy's predicament into consideration when I say that, either. This team is rock solid and the best team I've ever had the pleasure of working with, and that's down to you, both of you. I would see all that hard work unravel if we lost *you* in particular, Lorne," Anne stated with a slight smile.

Lorne thrust her shoulders back and exhaled a large breath. "No fear of that, ma'am. I'm in a totally different place personally than I was back then. My marriage to my first husband, Tom, was in tatters, for a start. I want to assure you that Tony and I have never really had a bad argument. Oops, have I just tempted fate there?" Everyone's laughter cut through the icy atmosphere that had cast a shadow over the room. "Charlie has recovered from the ordeal and is a vibrant, self-assured person now, too. Of course, I'd prefer keeping my family out of the situation altogether, but I'll ensure they're vigilant in their daily duties from now on. I don't think they'll want any protection, Sean. I'll certainly ask the question when I get home tonight, though, just to make sure."

"There's no need for reassurance on your part, Lorne. We're all aware of your capabilities at tackling difficult cases. All I ask is, if you feel things are getting on top of you, don't be afraid to shout out for help or advice. There's no 'I' in team. Remember that going forward, okay?" Anne said.

Lorne nodded. "I will. Anyway, let's see how this case develops first. We might be barking up the wrong tree."

"So, what did the caller say? How did he end the call? With high expectations?" Sean asked.

"Not really. He said that the 'fun' will begin at seven tomorrow. I better be here when he makes the call. Although, he did contact me via my mobile so it might not really matter where I am. It makes sense to be here rather than at home. I have a feeling he has a lot of running around lined up for me."

Sean smiled and turned his attention to Katy. "Okay, serious question to you, Katy. Are you going to be up for this? The only reason I ask is that you're looking awfully pale."

Katy shook her head. "Seriously, I don't have a clue. Providing there is a loo around, I should be okay. If not, then I'll be in the shit!"

"I think you should take a backseat, work alongside the rest of the team here at the station, while I work alongside Lorne."

Lorne's shoulders slumped, and a groan escaped her lips.

Everyone turned to look at her.

"Crap, really?"

Sean appeared stunned by her comment and seemed just about to open his mouth to object when she burst into laughter.

"Kidding! Just proving that I haven't lost my sense of humour," she added with a wink.

"Well, we did okay on the last case together. It would be good to team up again."

"If you say so, boss." Lorne said sarcastically, continuing to wind Sean up, until his glare bore into her. "Of course, I'm looking forward to it."

Anne clapped her hands together in one brief slap. "That's a deal then. I hear you two used to be a crack team when you both started out."

"We've had our ups and downs over the years, that's for sure," Sean stated, his face expressionless.

"That we have. Hopefully, any differences we've had over the years have been well and truly ironed out now. A lot of our issues revolved around your predecessor, ma'am," Lorne said.

"Well, at least you know where you stand with me, Lorne. Let's see if we can bring this case to a swift conclusion without anyone losing their lives, shall we? That'll be a novelty for your team, won't it?"

Lorne winced at her words. They were harsh but true, considering people usually died before the murder squad had reason to turn up. Lorne didn't think the super had meant for the words to come out the way they had. "We'll certainly do our best. Won't we, partner?" Lorne directed her question at the chief.

He nodded. "If there's nothing else, perhaps you ladies wouldn't mind leaving the super and me to get back to our meeting."

Katy and Lorne walked towards the door.

Lorne couldn't help firing another cheeky shot over her shoulder at him. "Don't forget to set your alarm early, boss. If I have to be here at seven, then it's imperative that my partner is here alongside me at the beginning of my shift." She left the room before he could respond.

Katy chuckled as she and Lorne made their way back to the incident room. "You're asking for trouble if you keep winding him up like that."

"Yeah, but it'll be worth it. He shouldn't be so easy to wind up."

"What's next?"

Lorne pushed through the door. "I don't want us to take this case for granted. I think we should spend the afternoon going through my old cases just in case we're wrong about the Unicorn element."

"We've got a couple of hours before the end of our shift. Why don't we pick a year each, work back the eight years to the present date."

"Great idea. The quicker we can come up with a positive ID for this Warrior chappie, the faster we can get the Hardys home safely. I'm trying to recall if I've ever had a case involving someone called Warrior, but nothing is coming to mind."

During the remainder of the shift, the team worked like an express train and established five possible names they could delve into the next day. All the people were still alive but confined to prison, not that it mattered. Villains could still carry on with their illegal activities from behind bars. Lorne studied the list to refresh her memories of each of the suspects and their crimes and whether they'd had partners who might have escaped Lorne's net. That was looking at things logically, of course. The Unicorn's face still popped up now and again to poke fun at her.

"Okay, that's sorted for tomorrow. Thanks for all your hard work, guys. You get off home. I have one vital call I want to make before I head off."

Everyone shut down their computers, quickly tidied their desks, and left. Only Lorne, Katy, and AJ remained.

"Are you ringing Hardy?" Katy asked, resting her weary body on the edge of the desk closest to Lorne's.

"Correct. He's got to play ball with us now." Lorne picked up the phone and dialled his office number.

"Hello," he answered.

"Mr. Hardy, this is…" Surprised he'd answered the call himself, she glanced up at Katy and winked. "Detective Inspector Lorne Warner. We met earlier today."

"Ah, yes. So you're now fully aware of the situation, I presume?"

"We are. I can totally understand your hesitation not to trust us earlier, given the circumstances. I hope that won't be the case going forward."

"I'll do anything that is necessary to bring my family home safely, Inspector. I'm going out of my mind with worry."

"I assure you, sir, my team won't let you down. We'll do everything in our power to bring your family home to you. I need to ask you a few questions, if I may?"

"Such as?"

"Can you shed any light on who we're dealing with? I know the man goes by the name of Warrior, but that's all I know."

"I have no idea. This has all come as a total shock for me."

"I hope you don't mind, but my partner and I took the liberty of scouting around your property today as we were in the vicinity, and I have to say one thing struck us as being very odd."

"Oh, what was that, Inspector?"

"Your lack of security. Can I ask why?"

"We've recently moved. I have it in hand, but the work isn't due to start for a week or two. The firm I'm using is supposed to be the best around, but they told me that a high volume of burglaries in the region lately has meant they have a backlog of contracts to fulfil before they get to mine."

"I see. That explains it perfectly. I'm sorry there was a delay."

"Me, too. The guilt is keeping me awake at night. All I can hear is a mantra playing over and over in my mind… 'if only.' Had I been fortunate enough to have a crystal ball in my possession, this terrible incident could have been avoided."

"There really is no point in blaming yourself, Mr. Hardy. Until we have proof otherwise, we need to look at this case as a spur-of-the-moment act, unless you can give us a reason to treat it as something else, that is?"

"I'm not with you."

"I need to ask if you've upset anyone enough for them to abduct your family."

"I'm in a high-risk business. Sometimes the need to use cut-throat tactics is high up on my agenda. I can probably name several hundred possible candidates if you're looking along those lines. I've been in this business for nearly fifteen years. As you can imagine, my enemies would stem back to the beginning of my career. Please, please don't ask me to name everyone whom I've ever fallen out with businesswise, because I'm sure I would find it an impossible task."

"I completely understand. Maybe I can ask you about deals you've carried out this year in that case. I'm not sure if you have partners in your firm or not. Perhaps one of them might be carrying a grudge. Anything along those lines? The more information we have at the beginning of the investigation, the better chance we have of catching the culprit, as I'm sure you can appreciate."

"I do appreciate that. The only person that really comes to mind is Jordan Richman."

"And who is that?"

"A former partner of mine. He screwed up a major deal we had a lot of money invested in. I was livid when the client sought out and signed a lucrative contract with one of our major competitors."

"Well, that would be a start. He'd certainly count as an interested party from our perspective. We'll make contact with him and bring him in for questioning. Do you have his address?"

"Wait a moment. Let me check his file." A drawer opened, and paper rustled. Then Hardy picked up the phone again. "He lives out in the sticks, travels into the city every day. His address is 28 Foxcroft Road, Leatherhead."

"Surrey? He travels in every day, you say? That's quite a commute."

"Yes, it's about an hour. He lives in a converted barn complex I think you'll find."

"Is there anything else you can tell me about him? Is he married?"

"Yes, wife and two small children. Would he really do something as vile as this if he had kids of his own?"

"Desperate people do desperate, and often, vile acts, Mr. Hardy. We'll look into Richman in the morning. In the meantime, if you can come up with some other names you might think would be of interest to us, I'd appreciate it."

"I'll do my best and ring you in the morning. I'm going home for the first time since my family was taken. Maybe a shower and a good night's sleep will help me cope with this ordeal better."

"That's the ticket. Try and rest when you can. I've had orders from this Warrior person to be at my desk at seven a.m. I'll be in touch soon. Don't worry; you will be informed of our progress along the way. Sleep well."

"Thank you and good luck."

Lorne hung up. "Can you delve into this in the morning, Katy? I think we'll need to pay Mr. Richman a visit at his residence. If he still works in London, he's sure to set off early."

"What if I can catch him at the office instead?"

"That's just it, I don't have a clue if he's found another job in the city or not. It's best to ring him first thing to find out. Maybe you and one of the boys can pay him a visit, while I'm otherwise occupied with Warrior."

"Makes sense. What also makes sense is us calling it a day now. I don't envy you having to tell Tony the news when you get home."

Lorne's mouth twisted. "Fingers crossed he'll be fine."

Charlie and Sheba, the German shepherd they'd recently welcomed into their home, were exiting the back door of the house when Lorne pulled into the drive.

"Hey, you, where are you off to?"

"Mum! I told you, we're inspecting that agility club."

"Of course, silly me. Sorry, sweetheart. I've had a pig of a day. Is Tony in?"

"He is." Charlie sniggered and kissed her mother on the cheek.

"Oh no. Don't tell me he's been experimenting in the kitchen again."

"Okay, I won't. But he has. Good luck," Charlie shouted over her shoulder. She placed Sheba in the back of the kennel's van and hopped behind the steering wheel.

Lorne watched her daughter drive out the gate and prayed for her safe return after the disturbing images that had resurfaced during the day. She didn't hear the door open behind her, and when Tony's arms wrapped around her, she squealed with fright. Turning quickly, she looked at him.

"Hey, that's not exactly the welcome I was hoping for, especially as we have the place to ourselves tonight with Charlie out on her doggy mission. Are you all right?"

"Let's go inside. I have something to tell you."

He backed up and muttered, "Crap! That sounds bloody ominous."

Lorne inhaled and exhaled a few silent breaths then smiled when she ordered him to sit at the kitchen table. "Can I switch off the dinner for a while?" she asked, surveying the bubbling pots on the stove.

He shrugged. "Do what you want. Looks like the beef I was cooking is off the menu anyway."

"You worry too much. I'm sure it'll be fine." She opened the oven door and was greeted with a plume of smoke that gave way to the blackened piece of topside she'd been looking forward to cooking for their Sunday roast. She switched off the oven, closed the door, and went to sit next to him. She leaned over and kissed his cheek. "I love you for at least trying to help out, hon. Not every man would think of cooking for his wife after a long day at work himself."

"Okay, now that you've softened me up, hit me with it." His face beamed with the brightest of smiles.

Again Lorne was reminded how lucky she was to share her life with him. They'd lived through so much anguish over the years after his tussle with the Taliban in Afghanistan. He'd been captured during a covert operation, and they had tortured him and ultimately cut off his leg. Tony had overcome the disability well, and instead of tearing their relationship apart, the adversity had only made it a thousand times stronger. Lorne had never loved her first husband,

Charlie's father, Tom, with as much intensity as she loved Tony. She had always said that she and Tony were true soulmates.

"Well, the first part I think you'll find interesting."

"Stop procrastinating and get on with it." He gripped her hand gently in his.

"Okay. I've been promoted... again!"

He laughed and shook his head. "And you think I'd be disappointed to hear you say that? I couldn't be more delighted for you, darling. You deserve to be an inspector, with all your experience."

Lorne's head fell onto the table as the huge breath left her body. She pulled upright again and saw the love shining in his eyes. "I'm so bloody relieved to hear you say that. I know we made promises at the start, when we first bought this place. I just feel I've negated on those promises."

"Don't be foolish. Hey, so what's going on with Katy? Is she leaving?"

"No. We're just swapping roles for now. That might change once the baby is born, but I somehow doubt it."

"Are you saying that you doubt she's going to find motherhood easy?"

"I'm not speaking ill of my friend. Don't put words into my mouth, hon. I'm just saying if she's struggling with morning sickness now, the odds are she's going to find dealing with a newborn a darn sight harder. Speaking from experience, it's bloody hard bringing up a child, a demanding role too many people in our society today take lightly. I'm not saying Katy hasn't thought things through properly, and I know that once the child is born, AJ is going to step in and take over, but I do wonder if they fully appreciate the demands involved in bringing up a child."

"Well, maybe this will be the making of them. Put it this way—it will either make them stronger or tear them apart."

Lorne shook her head. "I really didn't want to get into this tonight. I'm truly not speaking out of turn here, just telling it how it is. The poor girl is really struggling to cope with the important changes her body is going through. Anyway, that aside, I'm extremely glad and grateful to have your agreement on this. It means the world that you support my decisions."

"That's a given, Lorne. The same way that I appreciate your backing on me starting up the PI business you set up. We're a team, full stop. What's really going on here?"

"You know me so well. I'm incredibly lucky to have found you."

"Yeah, we go together like cheese and biscuits, salt and vinegar…"

"All right, enough of the food analogies." She swept a hand over her face. "Something happened at work today."

His brow furrowed, and his grip around her hand tightened. "Like what? A new case? Something to do with the team?"

"A new case. Oh hell, again, I'm just going to come out and tell you what's on my mind. Once it's out in the open, we can debate it, all right?"

"Of course. What's wrong, love?"

"I think the team's newest case has something to do with the Unicorn."

He withdrew his hand from hers and slumped back in his chair. Confused, he stated, "It can't be. He's dead. *You killed him!*"

"Tony, you don't have to tell me that. You know how I have a tendency to work on gut instinct? Well, right now, that instinct is super high, almost off the scale, to be honest."

"You better tell me the whole story. What's the case?"

She spent the next twenty minutes going over every detail of the case.

"Well, the similarities are there," he said. "I can't dispute that. I think you need to hold back those suspicions until you've had a chance to look into this Richman's background first and any other probable candidates that Hardy comes up with overnight. You say you've got to be at work at seven in the morning?"

"Yep, that's when the 'party' is going to begin."

"Eek, I don't envy you there."

Lorne fell silent, lost in her own convoluted thoughts until Tony left his chair and knelt on his good knee beside her, forcing her to look into his face.

"Whatever—and I mean whatever—shit comes our way, Lorne, we'll deal with it. Together. I'll always be here for you, no matter how much someone tries to come between us. We'll remain solid. Okay?"

She smiled and touched her forehead to his. "That really isn't my concern right now, Tony, although the guarantee you've just given me is very reassuring. It's Charlie I'm worried about. With us both out, she's a sitting target running this place by herself."

"By herself? Are you forgetting Carol's input? Hey, with her psychic powers, I predict Charlie will have a dozen guardian angels watching over her once Carol is aware of the problem. Maybe you should have a word with her, see if she can see any link to the Unicorn?"

"That's a great idea. I might call her after dinner. Okay, enough doom and gloom. How did your day go?"

He kissed her on the lips, walked back towards the cooker, and turned on the gas under the saucepans containing the vegetables once again. "Well, we finally managed to track down Shirley Black."

"That's brilliant news. Where was she?"

"Hiding out with her lover."

"Oops, not so brilliant news for the hubby then."

"Exactly. I don't need to tap into Carol's abilities to foresee what direction that marriage is heading in."

Lorne chuckled and crossed the room to join him. She placed an arm around his waist and stirred the gravy with the wooden spoon. "Has anyone told you lately what a wonderful wife you'd make?"

"Ha! What? Serving up burnt offerings every night? I suppose I should get my act together soon if you're going to accept that promotion."

"Are you sure you don't mind?"

"Did you seriously have doubts that I would, Lorne? I know you're an independent lady, on the verge of being stubborn most of the time, but I also know that your love for the Met ranks highly in your life. I'd be the dumbest fool around if I ever stood in your way over that, love."

"That's not quite how I would have put it myself. However, you have hit the nail on the head." She placed her hand over her heart. "I don't see my career as just that, never have really. You know how some writers and artists say their chosen career paths were a calling? I feel pretty much the same way. I was born to be a copper, to rid this world of the vilest of criminals. The trouble is, I don't ever think that will be accomplished in my lifetime."

"You sound like one of those superheroes—which one would you be now?" He thought over the options for a while then snapped his fingers. "I know! The Dark Angel of the Night."

"What? Are you serious? You make me sound like a superprossie!"

They both laughed raucously and together dished up the dinner.

After their passable meal had finished, Tony washed up the dishes and instructed Lorne to do what necessary paperwork she'd brought home, so that they could spend a few hours together curled up in front of the TV, making the most of their time alone.

Lorne didn't need telling twice. She went in the living room, removed two spare sheets of paper from the printer, and sat down at the kitchen table again. She wrote out a list of the names the team had gathered, covering all the angles in case her intuition about the Unicorn turned out to be wrong.

At the top of the list, she placed Bella Croft, whom she jailed after her involvement in the Internet dating case that had been thought up by, of all people, her sister Jade's psychiatrist. Lorne shuddered as she recalled her sister's lucky escape.

Then she noted down Felicity Randolph, who had formed a bizarre witches' coven under the guise of drawing together a team of women who'd been ill-treated by their partners to exact their revenge.

Next on the list was a powerful man, and upon reflection Lorne actually moved his name to the very top. Joseph Syposz had run a number of illegal businesses, which included forging residency documents for illegal immigrants.

She discounted Danny Smalling, the man guilty of killing his girlfriend, Noelle, who's spirit had led Carol to help convict him. Lorne didn't think he would have it in him to retaliate. The last names she added to the list were another truly probable couple who had used the foster care system in the UK to feed their lust for abusing children. But Courtney and Cathy Platt had proven to be only the tip of the iceberg.

After compiling the list, she jotted down a plan of action for her team to carry out the next day while she would be otherwise engaged with Warrior. The tasks included completing thorough background checks on Richman, sending Katy and another member of the team to question him, and getting Karen to ring around all the prisons where the listed suspects were residing at present, to see if there had been any kind of incidents lately involving those particular prisoners.

The only lingering doubt she had was what to do about the Unicorn scenario?

CHAPTER FIVE

Lorne woke after a fitful night's sleep to a beautiful dawn chorus. It was one of the main reasons she loved living out in the country. She stretched beside Tony, hugged and kissed his back, then leapt out of bed to take a shower. At six thirty, she crept downstairs only to find Charlie sitting at the kitchen table, eating a bowl of cereals.

"Wow, you're up early," her daughter said.

Lorne kissed the top of Charlie's head and made a mug of coffee, which she topped up with cold water so it was cool enough to down in a few gulps. "Busy day ahead. How did it go last night?"

Finishing a mouthful of cornflakes, Charlie replied, "Good. Sheba was fab. I think I'm going to enjoy it there."

"Ah! That's young person's lingo for 'I might have seen a nice boy there,' isn't it?" Lorne tapped the side of her nose with her finger.

Charlie's cheeks immediately flared up.

"No need to reply, sweetheart. Your face is telling me all I need to know."

Charlie poked her tongue out at her, and Lorne laughed.

"Okay, this conversation needs to be revisited when I get back tonight—if I get back, that is." She added the final part quietly.

Charlie wasn't easily fooled, though. "Oh? What's going on? A huge case?"

"Yep, very huge! I'll have to fill you in later, sweetheart. Stay vigilant throughout the day, as usual, okay?"

"Sure. But you can't just tell me that and run. What gives, Mum?"

"I really don't have the time, love. Just do as I ask. I think Tony will be hanging around today anyway."

"Now you're freaking me out. He's going to be here for my protection. Is that what you're getting at?"

"No! Look, Charlie. Just listen to me. Don't argue or try and analyse what I'm saying. I have to run. Love you loads." She ran out the kitchen door and jumped in the car. When she reversed and drove past the house, she saw an irritated Charlie standing at the back door with her hands on her hips. Lorne waved and blew her a kiss, which was not reciprocated. *Crap! The last thing I wanted to do was piss her off.*

Falling out with her daughter so early in the day didn't bode well for what lay ahead of her. She sighed constantly as she battled the commuters joining her, driving into London at this ungodly hour.

She arrived at the station and ran up the stairs to the incident room. Gasping for breath, she looked up at the clock on the wall. *6:58. Christ! That was a close shave.* The door opened behind her, scaring the crap out of her. "What the?"

"Yes, Inspector? Don't let me stop you. Surprised to see me at this time of day?"

She pulled a face at her superior. "I was just catching my breath, only just got here myself before the call comes in. And yes, I'm surprised to see you. Glad to see you're taking your role as my partner seriously, though."

"Of course. I know the consequences you'd likely dish out if I didn't."

Lorne's mobile rang, halting their ribbing each other. She took a few short breaths and then answered. "Hello."

"Ah, I do hope you are where you're supposed to be, *Inspector?* At the office and not at home."

"I am indeed, as instructed."

"Good. Then let us begin. When I said you'll have your work cut out for you over the next few days, I meant it. You will have thirty-six hours to come up with ten million in cash, used notes. Any sign of the notes being tampered with, and the kid gets it. Right?"

"Yes, you have my word on that. Where is this money coming from? Mr. Hardy?"

"How the fuck should I know? Just get it. For someone who is supposed to be the best detective in the Met, you ask some pretty stupid questions."

"I'm sorry. All I was asking in a roundabout way is whether Mr. Hardy was aware of the ransom demand or not."

"He's not. You are. Enough said. Do what you need to do to get that money. Now, listen very carefully. I want you to get in your car—take your mobile with you, of course—and head into the heart of the city."

"Any particular spot? It's a vast area."

Warrior laughed loudly in her ear. "Don't I know it? And so will you by the end of this adventure. I'll contact you again in twenty minutes. That should give you enough time."

"But…" Lorne tried to argue with him, but the line went dead. "Crap."

Sean had listened to the conversation close to Lorne's side. "Well, I'm coming with you."

"What? You can't do that."

"Did you hear him say anything about going it alone?"

She contemplated his question then shook her head. "No. Okay. I'm going to leave these notes here for Katy to deal with and then get on the road. Are you ready for this?"

"Ready or not, here we come. Twenty minutes doesn't give us much time. Maybe we can fool him into thinking we're closer if we get stuck in a traffic jam."

"I wouldn't take this guy lightly if I were you, Sean. You risk getting the Hardys killed."

"Okay, for your information, I was just teasing."

"My advice would be not to intentionally wind me up on this mission. I might not be responsible for my actions, and I would hate to be demoted the day after gaining my promotion."

Lorne quickly wrote a note and left it on AJ's desk, which was nearest to the door, then she bolted down the stairs, knocking several uniformed officers out of her way in her haste.

"Hey, slow down," Sean advised from fifty yards behind her as he tried his hardest to keep up with her.

"Here's a novelty suggestion for you to consider, boss; why don't you up a gear and push yourself? It would be great if you at least tried to keep up with me." She reached her car, turned, and smiled. She jumped in and revved the engine a few times impatiently while she waited for him to join her. She swiftly left the car park once Sean had secured his seatbelt in place.

"Do you want me to use the satnav, for the quickest route?" Sean asked.

She glanced his way with a look that questioned whether he was pulling her leg or not. He shrugged his innocence in return.

"I think I have this one in hand, boss. Thanks, all the same." She put her foot down harder than usual, her escalating pulse rate driving her actions more than she'd anticipated. Winding her way through the steady flow of traffic, she crunched through several of the gears and glanced sharply to look at Sean when he cursed under his breath. "Maybe *you* should drive once we arrive at our destination," she snapped back at him.

"That's a great idea. Why hadn't I thought of that?"

She quickly glanced back at him and scowled. They approached the outskirts of the city, with five minutes to spare. "Where do you suggest I head for?"

"Buck Palace is as good a place as any."

Her mobile rang before she could select the right gear and pull away again. "Where are you?" Warrior demanded.

"I was heading for Buckingham Palace."

"Forget that. Go to the Tower."

"What? The Tower of London?"

"You heard me. I'll give you twenty minutes, no longer, to get there."

"Jesus, do you think this car has got wings?" Lorne complained, eyeing the traffic building up around her.

He said nothing in response. However, Lorne heard mutterings then the distinctive muffled sounds of the baby crying. The sound grew louder the more the man spoke to the infant.

"Want to challenge me again, Simpkins?"

"No. There's no need to keep hurting the child."

"Hurt it. A light tap, and you think that's hurting the bloody thing? Maybe I should start breaking some limbs, see how the child reacts then. The ball's in your court, lady. Slip up, and that's exactly what's going to happen. Am I making myself clear?"

"Yes, very clear. I'm on my way now."

"Remember... the clock is ticking. Tick tock!"

His laughter chilled her to the bone as he ended the call. If ever there was an urgency to not foul up a case, it was evident every time Warrior issued a threat against the child.

"Keep focused, Lorne," Sean ordered as if picking up on her damning thoughts.

"I intend to. Right, it's off to the Tower."

It wasn't long before they had St. Paul's Cathedral in their sights. Lorne swallowed hard when she noted the time on her dashboard and the number of cars moving at a snail's pace in front of her. "I'm worried we're not going to make it. Damn, is that his intention? To ask the impossible of us? Is that what the next thirty-six hours are going to consist of?"

"Well, if it is, then between us, we'll ensure we're up for the challenge. If I remember rightly, the Tower is only about ten minutes from St. Paul's."

"Yeah, you're right, in light traffic maybe. I could always use my siren?"

"We've got plenty of time. I'd rather not panic the general public into causing a crash, if it's all the same to you, Inspector. The cars wouldn't be able to let us through anyway. If we need to use it later then that's a different story. Stop complaining and put your foot down."

Lorne pouted and shook her head at what seemed to be an impossible task. *Yep, when we stop, matey, you're definitely taking over the driving seat.*

The minutes ticked by agonisingly, but they still managed to reach their destination with a full minute to spare. Lorne sat there, with the engine still running, in the car park of the major tourist attraction and drummed her fingers on the steering wheel. "Where is he? Ring, damn you."

Sean chuckled. "Patience was never a strong suit of yours, was it?"

Another scowl descended, and Lorne punched him in the leg. "Boss or no boss, wisecracks are not permitted at this time." Her mobile rang, saving them both from further conflict. "Hello."

"You made it then. Good."

Lorne scanned the car park to see if there were any cars in the vicinity. There were a few cars in the car park, but all of them appeared to be empty. *That can't be right. He can't be here. That would mean he would have to take the child with him. Or he has a partner...* "Yes. I'm here."

"Right, here's where the treasure hunt begins. Go to the White Tower. Somewhere near the entrance will be an object out of keeping with its surroundings."

"Crap, you can't leave me dangling like that."

"Watch me! You have until eight ten to find it. That's thirty minutes."

Lorne stared at her phone for a split second after Warrior hung up. "Shit! We have to go. Any idea which tower is which?"

"No idea. I haven't been here for years. As London residents, we rarely visit the tourist sites, do you?"

"No, and that's not helpful." Lorne got out of the vehicle and slammed the door.

Sean moved around the car to stand beside her and withdrew his mobile from his pocket. "Let's see if we can get the info from the net."

"Can you do that while we walk? We're wasting time, and the countdown has begun." Lorne impatiently trotted off towards the vast and intimidating castle.

"Of course. It says here that the Tower dates back to the eleventh century. Holy crap, that's over a thousand years old."

"Oh, great. By the end of the day, you'll be an expert tour guide. Any chance you can throw some water on your enthusiasm there, Sean?"

"Sorry. This is interesting stuff."

"Yeah, for tourists, not for investigating officers trying to track down a suspect holding a woman and her child captive."

"Okay, I hear you. Keep your hair on. I'll save that page for later."

Luckily for Lorne, she had chosen to wear trainers instead of the mid-height heels she usually favoured to wear at work. She ran ahead of Sean, turned, and urged him to keep up.

He was struggling to run while looking down at his mobile.

"Sean, for Christ's sake," she shouted back at him. *I'm beginning to wonder if I would have been better off doing this alone.*

"Whoa! Anne Boleyn was beheaded with an axe in this very tower."

Lorne frowned and dug deep into her memory for something she'd heard regarding that fact on TV a few years ago. "I think you'll find that was reported incorrectly at one point. She was actually beheaded by a sword, not an axe."

He chortled. "You're good. I was testing you. I didn't know that Guy Fawkes was tortured and interrogated here, though. That's amazing." He shuddered. "All that history, if walls could speak, eh?"

Lorne inwardly cursed and shouted over her shoulder, "Sean, back in the car, you told me to remain focused. Now I'm begging you to do the same. Otherwise, you might as well return to base. Harsh words—I know—but true."

"All right. I'm just throwing out some facts while we work, interesting facts, at that."

Lorne raised her arms out to the side and slapped them against her thigh. "I frigging give up. Button it and get a move on," she shouted, incensed. She heard Sean mumble some kind of apology and heard his footsteps pick up pace behind her. Finally, he caught up with her.

"Right, we're here. His instructions were to look around for something that is totally out of place in its surroundings."

"That's a tad cryptic, isn't it?"

"I doubt this guy has plans to make this exercise a breeze. I think we should split up and take a section at a time."

"I think it would be wiser for us to search the same area and then move onto the next one. It'll save time."

"Is that how it's going to be, Sean? I say one thing, and you suggest the total opposite? We do things my way, okay? I'm in charge of this investigation. You're only tagging along for the ride, pretending to be my partner, right?"

He ignored her comment and searched the immediate area close to the Tower's walls.

Lorne was grateful he didn't retaliate. The last thing she needed was a sulking chief inspector hanging around her neck. She scanned the area a few feet away from her partner and asked, "Anything?"

"Nope. I'm moving on."

They both took a few steps to their right and continued to repeat the process for the next ten infuriating minutes. "This is bloody impossible. There's such a vast area to search, it's pointless."

"Call him back. His number has registered, hasn't it?"

"Nope. I didn't expect him to be that dumb. He's probably using a pay-as-you-go phone to keep us on our toes. Let's move areas and widen the gap between us."

They had worked their way along one side of the tower and had three remaining walls to check. Nearing the end of the stone wall, Lorne spotted something in a clump of long grass close to the end turret. "Here, what do you reckon, Sean?"

He looked down at the yellow object and nodded. "It has to be."

Lorne grabbed the plastic yellow duck and picked it up. Her mobile rang immediately. "Hello."

"It took you long enough, Simpkins."

"I've got it. What do you want me to do with it?"

"Chuck it in the nearest bin then get back to the car and head for Marble Arch."

"Are you kidding me? We've just come from that direction."

"And whinging like that ain't gonna help your cause, lady. Now get cracking. I'm going to be more generous and give you a full forty-five minutes to get there. However, don't take me for a fool. I won't be so thoughtful at other locations."

"Thanks," she said grudgingly. "What should I look for when I arrive?"

"Go to the Marriot Hotel and await further instructions."

"On my way now," she said. However, the line was already dead.

"Where to now?" Sean asked, trotting after her as they made their way back to the car.

"The Marriot Hotel, and you're driving. My car that is, as well as driving me nuts."

"Ha! Bloody, ha! I'm a better driver than you anyway, so I'm sure your car will be pleased for the respite."

Lorne's eyes narrowed when she turned to look at him. "If it keeps you off that damn phone, I'm willing to cave on that one."

CHAPTER SIX

Katy and AJ pulled up at Jordan Richman's house. They were early, hoping to catch him before he had the chance to set off for work.

"That's a good sign. His car is still here." AJ pointed to the BMW convertible sitting on the drive.

Katy chuckled. "What's the betting that belongs to his wife?"

AJ raised his eyebrow. "On second thoughts, you're probably right. Nice car all the same."

"You mean you wouldn't mind adding it to your collection?"

AJ grinned. "One more wouldn't hurt, would it?"

Katy rubbed her tummy. "You have other responsibilities to take care of now, sweetheart, in case you've forgotten. I think the boys' toys will have to take a back seat until this one is a few years older."

AJ sighed. "Yeah, and there was me thinking I had my whole life ahead of me."

Katy pulled a face, letting him know how much his words had hurt.

He gently dug her in the ribs. "I'm joking. I wouldn't change the situation for all the caviar in Russia."

Katy gagged. "Did you have to mention food?"

"Sorry." AJ knocked on the door to the huge converted barn that was part of a complex consisting of four houses, set back off the small village road within a beautiful setting of open countryside at the rear.

A smartly dressed woman in her early thirties opened the door. "Can I help you?"

Katy and AJ flashed their warrant cards.

"We'd like a quick word with Mr. Richman if he's at home," Katy told the woman.

"Well, he's not. He works in the city and has to set off early." The woman bristled with annoyance.

"Can you give us an address where he can be contacted?" Katy smiled at the woman.

Her eyes narrowed into suspicious splits. "Why? Why do you want to speak to him?"

"We have a few questions, nothing major, we need to ask him. It's really just to help us with our enquiries."

"Into what?"

Katy intentionally remained evasive in case the woman got it into her head to ring and warn her husband they were on the way. "About a traffic incident that occurred the other day."

"He never mentioned anything about that. Are you sure you have the right person?"

Katy's smile never faltered. "Yes, absolutely sure. If you can give us the address?"

The woman tutted, left the front door open, and walked back into the house, her high heels clicking and echoing in the tiled hallway. She returned a few moments later with a slip of paper on which she had noted down her husband's work address and phone number. "Here you are. I'll ring him on his mobile, let him know that you're on your way."

Katy nodded. That was *not* what she'd wanted to hear. If Richman had abducted Hardy's family, then he might abscond if warned. "You're very kind. Thank you."

Katy and AJ returned to the car.

Once inside, AJ said, "Shit! What if he gets scared and takes off?"

Katy sighed and started the engine. "Precisely. I predict Richman not showing up for work today, don't you? I hope for our sakes that I'm wrong about that, but I doubt it."

They drove into the city and located the address without much hassle. Katy parked in the underground car park below the office building, and she and AJ rode the lift to the twentieth floor.

Katy flashed her ID at the receptionist. "We're here to see Mr. Richman. Is he in?"

The bespectacled woman frowned and looked at the appointment book in front of her. "Is he expecting you?"

"No. It's official police business," Katy said.

"Just a moment, please." The receptionist left the desk and knocked lightly on the door behind her.

"Come in," a voice boomed, and the woman slipped inside the office.

Katy raised an eyebrow and whispered, "Okay, this looks promising."

The door opened again, and the receptionist reappeared, accompanied by a slim, suited man of around six feet, eyeing them both suspiciously.

"You wanted to see me, Sergeant Foster?" he asked impatiently.

"Yes, in private, if you don't mind?" Katy replied.

"Come into my office. Can I offer you a drink?"

"No, we're fine. Thanks all the same."

AJ followed Katy into the man's executive office. One of the walls was lined with bookshelves full of leather-bound reference books. Katy suspected there were probably a few first-edition copies included in the display. Another wall consisted of floor-to-ceiling glass, and the view over the city took Katy's breath away for an instant. She could imagine the scene at night, all the varying shapes and sizes of London's historical buildings lit up and glistening amidst the midnight sky.

"Take a seat. What's this about, Sergeant?" he asked, tucking himself securely behind his highly polished mahogany desk.

"We're looking into an incident regarding a former colleague of yours."

"Oh, and who might that be?"

"Lance Hardy."

His frown deepened, but Katy didn't feel as if the man's reaction pointed to him knowing anything about the case. There again, it was possible that he attended a local amateur dramatic society and gained the ability to act surprised when the need arose.

"Are you telling me that you don't recognise the name, Mr. Richman?"

"Oh, I recognise it all right. What I don't understand is where this conversation is leading, Sergeant."

"Then I'll fill you in. First of all, I need you to clarify why you are no longer in business with Mr. Hardy."

"Ah, I get it. That's police talk to see if our stories match, am I right?"

"You're very smart, Mr. Richman. So?"

He relaxed back in his chair, not showing any signs of stress or aggravation.

"So. He accused me of screwing up a major deal for *our* company."

"And did you?" Katy asked.

"These things happen in business, big business. He was on holiday at the time with his family. I suppose I was an easy target to apportion the blame."

"So why did you leave the partnership?"

"It was an issue of trust. I trusted him, but it wasn't reciprocated. Yes, we lost a lot of money on that deal. I'm talking millions of revenue here. But it was no different to the deal he screwed up a few months before."

"I see. So you felt hard done by. Is that what you're saying?"

"Not exactly. The kind of business we deal in—imports and exports, that is—well, there's always some idiot out there prepared to undercut the big boys. And yes, I regarded our firm as one of the big boys. Sometimes you just have to swallow your pride and move on to bigger and greater things."

"And you're saying that Mr. Hardy didn't see it that way?" Katy asked.

"Indeed. It was a case of 'I can screw up, but when you do it, that's totally unforgiveable.' I got tired of all the grief he directed at me and told him to buy me out."

"Which he did, right?"

Richman nodded. "Yes, without any ensuing slanging match. The whole deal was sorted out within a week."

"And you found this job quite quickly after you finished working there?" Katy asked as AJ jotted down the man's answers in his notebook.

A smile broke out on his face. "This is my new business, Sergeant. I could never work for anyone else after running my own business for years."

"I see. So are you telling me that you're now in direct competition with Mr. Hardy?"

"I am."

"Is that even ethical? Isn't there some kind of law about starting up the same sort of business within a certain number of miles of your preceding one?"

"There is, and I think you'll find that this office is just outside of that range, Sergeant."

"That's good to know, and since setting up this business, have you and Mr. Hardy crossed paths at all?"

"No. There's no necessity for that to ever happen. What exactly is going on here? Am I allowed to know?"

"We're investigating a major crime. I'm sorry, I can't go into further detail at the present."

"Major crime involving Hardy? I don't understand. Has he done something illegal?"

"Not exactly, no," Katy replied cagily.

He flung his arms up in the air. "Then I have to tell you that you're not making any sense. Are you insinuating I'm involved in this 'major crime' somehow?"

Katy scratched her forehead. "We're looking into the crime from all angles. At this moment in time, that's all I'm willing to divulge."

"Well, unless you're willing to enlighten me on what has gone on, I don't see what further use I can be to you. So if you'll excuse me, I have a meeting to attend first thing with a client."

"Okay, thank you for your time. There may be a need to question you in the future if things progress and more information comes to light. Can I count on you coming down the station for an interview should that occur?"

"Of course." He showed them to the door and shook their hands.

"What do you make of him?" AJ asked after he and Katy had stepped into the elevator.

Katy, feeling a little queasy due to the swift descent, shrugged in response. Once they'd left the lift, she said, "At this point, I'm not sure what to think of him. He seemed rather cool, wouldn't you say?"

"I agree. It could be a sign of his innocence, though, right?"

"It could mean a lot of things. We'll bear him in mind as the case continues. We should get to the station, maybe contact Lorne to see what's going on with her."

***

Warrior paced the floor, constantly keeping one eye on his watch and the other on the woman feeding her child in front of him. "Isn't he full yet?" He leaned forward and yelled in her ear.

Bethany cowered away from him and clutched her baby tighter in her arms. "He's a growing lad. He needs regular feeding, which you're not allowing me to give him. Please, let me stay up here. If you keep me locked away, my baby will be neglected. He's young, needs his mother near him for reassurance."

He leaned in again and raised his hand, ready to hit her. She flinched and shied away. "Less of telling me what I should and shouldn't do, lady, you hear me? This isn't some kind of effing holiday camp."

"I know, I'm sorry. I won't do it again, I swear."

"Yeah, right. I'm betting you'll be tempted to have the same conversation tomorrow morning, too. Well, I'm warning you, *don't*. Or I'll do something to the sprog, right?"

"I understand. I'm sorry."

He ignored her once his watch registered 8:53. He hit the redial button on his phone. "Simpkins, you there yet?"

"Yes, I'm just going up the steps to the Marriot Hotel now."

"You're going to be late," he taunted.

"Please, give me a few minutes' grace. The traffic was at a near standstill on the way over here."

"Just this once, as I'm feeling generous. I'll call back in two minutes. I want you to locate the restaurant. If you're not at the restaurant by then, either the kid or the mother will suffer a broken bone or two."

"Don't! I'm almost there now," Lorne shrieked.

He hung up and sniggered. "I love sending you women in a flap. Don't think that I won't ever make good on my threats. This woman detective has both of your lives in her hands. If she screws up, I'll have no hesitation in finishing you both off. Yes, ten mill is at stake, but there'll be other opportunities for me to get my hands on that kind of dosh." He hit the dial button again, and Lorne picked up before the first ring ended.

"I'm here."

He grunted. "Are you sure?"

"Yes. What do you want me to do?"

He laughed at the out-of-breath inspector. "Right, listen very carefully. I worked hard on this cryptic clue. You have thirty minutes to find it."

"Okay."

"Food from every nation around the world, but the clue you are seeking is from these shores."

"Christ, is that it?"

"Yes. You have until nine to find it. If you don't, you know what I'll do."

"I'm on it now."

CHAPTER SEVEN

Lorne hung up and frantically searched the outside of the restaurant. "How the hell am I supposed to work this out, Sean?"

"We'll do it together, Lorne. Stay calm."

"Does he mean the clue relates to something inside the restaurant or out here? Can we even get inside at this time of day?"

"I should think so. I'll ask at reception?"

"No wait." She clasped his arm, preventing him from leaving her. "Of course we can get inside." She tried the door and found it locked. "There must be another entrance. I've never heard of a hotel restaurant not serving breakfast, have you?"

"You're right." Sean ran to the end of the corridor then drew her attention by whistling. "Over here."

Lorne joined him, and they rushed into the room set out for a breakfast sitting. Lorne scanned the area; only three tables were occupied by hotel guests, who all looked their way with enquiring glances when they barged into the room. She pointed at the buffet-style breakfast. "We should see what food they're serving up."

Sean started at one end of the line while Lorne began at the other, and they met in the middle. "What do you think?" Sean whispered.

"It has to be under the English breakfast dishes, yes?"

"Okay, but how would he get anything *under* the dishes. Isn't that a bit obvious?"

Lorne tutted. "I don't know, Sean. I'm open to all suggestions or bright ideas. Feel free to chip in when the need takes you."

"Now don't start taking your frustrations out on me, Inspector."

She sighed. "Sorry. I'm bound to be a bit tetchy. Just ignore me."

A young female chef appeared behind the counter, holding a plate in her hand. "Good morning. What can I get for you?"

"Sorry, we're not waiting to be served." Lorne flashed her warrant card. "Is there a manager around who we can talk to?"

The woman placed the plate back on the pile and raised a finger. "I'll just get him for you."

She returned with a man in his early thirties, wearing a tall chef's hat. "Can I help you? You couldn't have interrupted me at a worse time, so if you wouldn't mind being quick, I'd appreciate it."

"Sorry, we realise you're busy." Lorne glanced over her shoulder at the meagre occupancy of the restaurant. "I just need to ask a few questions."

The man smiled briefly and clarified his previous statement. "The rush is about to happen any minute."

"And we're on a deadline to save two people's lives, so if you'll just bear with us for a few minutes."

"Okay, you've got my attention." The man stepped closer to the counter and rested his hands on the metal shelf.

"We've been given a clue from someone regarding this restaurant. We think it has to do with the English breakfast you're serving. Will you allow us to take a peek under your serving dish?"

"Of course." He lifted the silver dish off the hotplate.

Lorne inspected the area only to find the element and nothing else. "Hmm... okay. Well that's scuppered that idea."

"Anything else you wanted to ask? I really need to get on, Inspector." the chef asked, replacing the dish.

"We have this clue: 'food from every nation around the world, but the clue you are seeking is from these shores.' Hence me thinking it had a connection with the English breakfast. Any ideas?"

The chef shook his head. "I'm sorry. I've never been one for crosswords. That does seem to be a very cryptic clue."

Lorne nodded. "Thanks for your help. If we promise to keep out of the customers' way, would you mind if we continue to search the restaurant?"

"Feel free. Sorry I couldn't be more help." The man smiled and returned to the kitchen.

Lorne faced Sean and shrugged. "What next?"

"I have no idea. Let's think about the clue logically."

"I have—over and over, and still, nothing is coming to mind."

"Then we'll have to search every corner of this restaurant before it gets any busier."

Lorne nodded. "I agree. The question is, Sean, what the hell are we looking for?"

"I'm sure it will become obvious once we find it. Until then, I'll go from left to right, okay?"

They separated, and under the watchful eye of the patrons already seated at the tables and any new arrivals coming into the restaurant, they began their search. Lorne picked up everything she could find on each of the vacant tables, but it was useless. She was nearing the edge of her designated search area when she heard Sean call her name.

She rushed over to him. The smug look on his face made her want to slap it. "Stop milking it, boss. What have you found?"

"See for yourself." He pointed at the menu on the table they were standing alongside.

Lorne picked it up and found a keyring attached to it. "A keyring? What's that all about?"

Sean shrugged. "I guess we'll find out once Warrior rings you." He glanced at his watch. "Which should be anytime soon."

Lorne went up to the girl behind the counter. "I'm taking this as evidence, okay?"

"Sure. I'll let my boss know. Glad you found what you were looking for."

Lorne and Sean walked down the steps of the hotel. "Come on, ring, you bastard." As if Warrior had heard her, her mobile rang. *Is he watching us? No, he can't be. He's at a location with the woman and child.* "Hello."

"Got it?"

"Yes. I'm confused, though. It's just a keyring," Lorne replied, surveying the immediate area to see if they were being observed by anyone. If not the abductor he might have an accomplice following and watching them. No one stood out amongst the commuters on their way to work.

"You're supposed to be. All will become apparent over the next thirty-six hours. How are you standing up to the task, Inspector?"

"Don't concern yourself with my well-being. Let's get on with things."

He snorted. "Eager, aren't you? I have a feeling you're the kind of person who doesn't appreciate being out of control of a situation. Am I right?"

"Tell me who wouldn't feel the same way I do in my current situation."

"Granted. Right, here's an easy trek for you. Make your way over to Hamleys Toy Shop. Got that? I hope you recognise how nice I'm being. Get it while you can, sweetheart. Things will become more difficult as the day progresses."

"You think this is easy? Battling the traffic at this time of the day, are you crazy?" Lorne bit down on her tongue, knowing she shouldn't have tried to goad the kidnapper.

"Feisty bitch. Mind you, I have been warned about that." He laughed and hung up.

"Quick, we need to get back to the car."

"Did he give you a time limit on this trip?" Sean asked, trotting after Lorne back to the car.

"No. Which makes me suspicious. We need to get on the road ASAP."

Sean opened the car, jumped behind the steering wheel, and set off.

Lorne held her hand out. "Give me your phone. I'll ring the station, see if Katy has arrived yet." He threw the phone in her lap. "Hi, Katy. It's me."

"Lorne, I didn't recognise the number. How's it going?"

"I have a feeling, by the end of our stint, we're going to feel like we've been slowly tortured to within an inch of our lives."

"Agh... that bad. Anything we can do to help from this end?"

Lorne thought for a second. "Actually, I'm calling for an update of how you got on with Richman. However, now you've raised the point, I think we should sort the team into shifts. I need to have someone on hand in the incident room twenty-four-seven. Can you arrange that?"

"Sure. What about the overtime? Can we afford it?"

Lorne turned to look at Sean, who was busy lane hopping, manoeuvring the car through a gap in the traffic. "I'm sure the chief will agree to that in this instance. He's a little busy right now to confirm it."

"Yes, I agree," Sean shouted to Lorne's amusement.

"Ooo... so you *can* multi-task after all." She giggled then straightened her face again when she renewed her conversation with her true partner. "This guy is taking pleasure in making us run the length and breadth of London. We're already en route to our third location of the morning."

"Shit! Right, I'll make this short. AJ and I set off early to try and catch Richman at home; we were too late. We caught up with him at the office instead. Didn't really get anywhere. To me, he seemed surprised by the events unfolding. No sign of recognition, leading me to think he has nothing to do with the crime. I don't think we should discount him out of hand just yet, though."

"I agree. Look, someone is either pulling this guy Warrior's strings, or he's plucked up the courage to abduct the Hardys off his own back. I'm inclined to believe it's the former. We need to chase up any CCTV footage regarding the car he pinched. Can you sort that for me?"

"Sure. What about calling a press conference. Shall I organise that, too?"

Lorne nodded and clicked her tongue. "Yeah, go for it. Someone might know where the car is or the route it took. At the moment, we have no idea. That car is going to be the key to this investigation."

"That's what I think, too. Let's get it out in the open as soon as poss. Want me to run that past Hardy first or just go ahead?"

"Maybe it would be wiser to ring him. Perhaps he'll volunteer to show up to make a personal plea for his family's safety."

"I'll do that. Will you check in regularly?"

"If I'm able to, yes. Sean's taking the pressure off me a bit by driving to each location."

"What if the kidnapper asks you to take the underground at some point?"

"Then we'll figure that out, if and when, it happens. Let me know via Sean's mobile how things go at your end, okay? We need to stay abreast of things, Katy. The bastard has already showed us his intent by making the baby cry. I dread to think what he'd do to the little mite if he really wanted to get his point across."

"The bastard. There's no chance of us taking this lightly at this end; you have my word on that. Be in touch soon. Be careful."

"Thanks. Good luck, hon."

Lorne ended the call and tipped her head back against the headrest. "I'm already bloody knackered."

"I have a feeling that is this guy's intention, Lorne."

"Mind if I ring Tony at home?"

"Sure, we're about fifteen minutes from our destination."

She paused to remember her home number. When she used her own phone, all she had to do was hit one, and the phone dialled it automatically. "Hey, Tony. Everything all right?"

"Yep, I was just thinking about you. How's it going there?"

"Exhausting, and we've only just begun."

"Crap! Well, don't worry about us; we're fine. I've run through everything with Charlie, and she said to pass on a message not to worry about her. She'll be extra vigilant during the day."

"Gosh! Was she all right about that? I avoided telling her at breakfast this morning."

"She's fine. You worry too much. She did ask if it would be okay for her to go to the agility club again this evening, though."

Lorne's interest piqued. "Again? Why so soon? Do you think she's met someone? I tried to worm it out of her this morning but didn't get very far."

"By the way she's been going around whistling this morning. I'd say you're on the right lines. Look, going back to your investigation, I know I've said it already, but I'm here if you need me. Don't forget, both Joe and I can call on extra resources from 'the mob' if you need a hand."

"Thanks. For the time being, I think we'll just go with the flow. I have a suspicion this guy has all manner of weird and wonderful things he'll want to challenge us with later on. You'll be the first number on my list if things escalate out of our control, okay?"

"Right, when have I heard that before?" he replied, sounding a little disgruntled.

"I'll be in touch soon. Love you."

She hung up and glanced sideways at Sean.

Her boss was smirking and mimicked her. "Love you!"

"Shut up and drive. It's good to know he's willing to lend us a hand if needed, eh?"

"We'll stick with our own options first, I think. Let's play this by the book where we can, all right?"

"Yep, I agree. I was just stating a fact."

Sean pulled into Regent Street and drew up outside the world famous toy store at 10:15. "Damn, where the hell are we going to park?"

"See if you can find a friendly traffic warden perhaps. Not my problem," she said, getting out of the car.

"Lorne, wait there. Do not move," Sean ordered out the driver's window.

However, Lorne pushed open the glass door to the toy store and rushed inside. At the base of the escalator, she had no idea what direction she should be going in, as Warrior hadn't informed her during his last call. As if reading her mind, the man rang her mobile.

"Hello, I'm here."

"Good. Glad to see that you can arrive at your given location efficiently, with or without time constraints, Simpkins."

"It's Warner, not Simpkins," she objected, distracted by her bustling surroundings.

"You're Simpkins to me. It suits my purpose to think of you as Lorne Simpkins. I know you married that MI6 agent and that you took him on in spite of his gammy leg."

Lorne gasped. "You know? Who are you? Have we met?"

"Ah, always the inquisitive copper. You'll find that out soon enough when our paths finally cross."

"How are the woman and her child holding up?"

"I think you're forgetting who's in charge here, *Simpkins*. Now quit gabbling on and listen. Go to the first floor. You're looking for Serengeti. It will be the key to your success."

The line went dead before she could say anything else. She almost jumped out of her skin when she felt someone tap her shoulder.

Breathless, Sean leaned over with his hands on his knees. "You could have waited."

She grabbed his arm and ran towards the escalator. "We have to get up to the first floor. Am I right in thinking that Serengeti is in Africa?"

"It was the last time I heard, unless it's moved of course. Why?"

"Warrior told me to go to Serengeti, metaphorically speaking, I believe, and the key to our success would be there."

The second Lorne stepped off the escalator, she realised the extent of the mammoth task ahead of them. "Jesus, the whole bloody floor is like a scene from *Out of Africa*. Where the heck do we begin?" Lorne heaved a large sigh.

"At the beginning. Are you sure he didn't hint at a certain area?"

"What, like he did with the menus you mean? Think about it, Sean, this guy's sole intention appears to be to give us the bloody run around."

"Maybe not his sole intention, Lorne, but I hear what you're saying."

"I had a chance to tackle him about using Simpkins instead of Warner, and he seems to know an awful lot about me and my private life, hinting that we have indeed met before. That reminds me—the next time I talk to Katy, nudge me to tell her to look into the villains on that list. The quicker we start eliminating suspects, the better. Let's go hunting!"

"What are we hunting for?" Sean asked.

"I don't know, perhaps a key to go with the keyring already in our possession."

"Sounds plausible. Want to split up again? You take that side of the room, and I'll take this?"

"Good idea. Shout when you think you've found something, and I'll do the same."

"Did Warrior say how long he's giving us to find the clue?" Sean asked.

Lorne frowned and shook her head. Then she quickly scanned the area, still under the assumption that someone might be following them. "No, strange. Isn't it?"

"We should crack on in case he surprises us by ringing in ten minutes or something. He's bound to try and keep us on our toes."

"Okay. You start searching while I have a word with the assistant. She might have seen someone hanging around acting strangely."

She left Sean to wander off to the other side of the display and approached the young assistant unpacking a box at the counter. The young, freckled girl in her late teens smiled broadly and asked, "Can I help, madame?"

She fished out her ID and showed it to the woman as she spoke. "We're dealing with a huge case at the moment, and our investigation has led us to this floor. Can you tell me if you've noticed anyone hanging around here in the last few days, acting suspicious?"

The girl chewed on her lip. "Yikes, lots of people mill around the display. Not sure they actually look suspicious while looking at stuffed toys, though. Sorry I can't be more helpful than that."

"Never mind, it was worth a shot. My partner and I will be searching the area if that's okay?"

"Sure. Can I help at all? Do you know what you're actually looking for?"

Lorne shrugged. "That's just it—no, we don't. But thanks for the offer."

"Just give me a shout if you need a hand."

Lorne smiled at the woman and headed for the stuffed giraffe section. Some of the creatures dwarfed her and were an incredible seven feet tall. She could imagine only rich people being able to afford to pay the two-thousand-pound price ticket as a gift for their kids. Lorne tried not to disrupt the display too much, but every now and again, one of the flimsier animals toppled to the ground. Embarrassed, she glanced over at the shop assistant, who giggled and looked the other way, while Lorne quickly reassembled the display in case the girl called security and requested their removal.

Waving to get Sean's attention, she mouthed, "Anything?"

"Nothing," he mouthed back, shrugging his disappointment.

They searched the entire section from the floor displays to the numerous shelves lining the walls without success.

Sean joined her. "What are we going to do now?"

"If only I had his number, I could ring him back." She continued to scan the area as they contemplated their next move. Something hanging from the ceiling glinted and caught her eye. She rushed over and stood beneath the nursery light that featured a scene from a safari. "Here. Lift me up, Sean."

Lorne was thankful that she'd decided to wear a pair of jeans to accompany her trainers for the occasion. Her boss grabbed her around the thighs and hoisted her up, groaning unexpectedly beneath her. "Christ, when did you put on so much weight? I don't remember you weighing this much when we dated."

Lorne unhooked the key. "Let me down. I've got it." When her feet hit the ground, she clouted Sean across the chest. "Cheeky bugger! I'll have you know that I'm the same weight now as when we dated all those years ago."

"Liar," he muttered. "A key, eh? I wonder what it opens."

Lorne glared at him through narrowed eyes and made a mental note to pay him back for his offensive comment once the case was over. "I'm sure Warrior will be ringing us soon with further instructions. For now, I'll slip it onto the keyring. We should get back to the car in case he rings." They ran down the escalator and out of the building. "Where did you park my car?"

"Round the back of the store on double yellows. I hope there's not a traffic warden waiting for us."

"Jesus, I don't suppose you thought to stick the police light on the roof of the car just in case, did you?"

He cringed. "Sorry. I didn't think."

"Paper-pusher brain in action, I see." They marched to the end of the building, and when they reached the back alley, Lorne's heart skipped a beat. "Damn and blast. Right, leave this to me. I'll have to flash him more than my ID to get us out of this fix."

Sean chuckled in spite of his straight face. "He's all yours."

Lorne sashayed up to the young traffic warden and smiled enthusiastically. "Hello there. I'm sorry. It was a police emergency." She showed him her ID.

"Not my problem. You guys know the rules better than anyone."

"Really, you're going to give me a ticket for carrying out police duties."

The warden continued to note down Lorne's car details. "Rules are rules. You're damn lucky I didn't get around to calling the tow-truck."

Lorne raised her arms then slammed her palms against her thighs. "Christ, we're busting our bloody guts to try and save a woman and her son's lives, and you're pulling your jobsworth act on me."

A brief smile of satisfaction tugged at the young warden's lips. "Yep. I have targets to meet. Besides that, you have deliberately parked in a no-parking zone. Maybe you should refresh your reading skills." He tore off the ticket, thrust it in a plastic wallet, and slapped it on the windscreen of the car.

Lorne seethed, and her eyes bulged as she struggled to find the words for a quick retort. Sean came to her rescue. "It was my fault. Like the Inspector told you, we're on an important case, and lives are in danger."

"Thems the breaks. Good day to you both. A word of advice: next time, read the signs carefully. And here's another tip for you: watch out for the double yellow lines, too. They have a habit of biting folks in the arse."

Lorne took a step forward, but Sean restrained her. The warden tipped his hat and bade them farewell.

"Of all the pig ignorant… what's his name? I'll make sure we pick him up on a speeding charge or something," she threatened, her cheeks flaming the more irate she became.

"Let it go, Lorne." Sean laughed and jumped in the car. Lorne joined him before he threw a further insult at her, "You're obviously losing your touch in your old age." He kept his eyes on the alley ahead and started the engine.

Lorne crossed her arms and looked out the window. At the end of the alley, her mobile rang again, adding to her foul mood. She swallowed her anger and answered brightly, "Hello. We found the clue. What's next?"

"You're getting good at this, Simpkins. Let's see if we can make the next clue a little more cryptic to up the pressure. I've made this too simple for you. I was expecting you to be more stressed about your adventure."

Lorne exhaled noisily. "If only you knew," she mumbled.

"Oh, I know," Warrior retorted, laughing. "Okay, drive to Soho. You're looking for a certain establishment, The Happy Cock."

Lorne groaned.

"What's the matter, Simpkins, don't you approve of your next destination?"

"No. But I have a feeling you're not going to be concerned about that."

"Bull's-eye! Got it in one, lady. You've got exactly fifteen minutes."

"What? We'll never make it; not in this traffic."

"'*We*'? Did you say 'we'?"

Lorne punched her thigh in frustration. She'd been careful not to let on about Sean. After thinking fast, she confessed, "Yes, we. But then you knew that already, didn't you? I know you have a pair of eyes out here reporting back to you. Grant me with some sense."

"Yes, I knew. I was just seeing if you had the decency to own up to your inept actions. From here on, you're going it alone, you hear me? Dump your boss and find your own way from now on. Got that?"

Lorne heard the baby crying in the background.

"Okay, you've got your wish. I'm ordering him out of the car now. Don't hurt the child, please. It was stupid of us to underestimate you."

"You've got that right. This is your final warning, lady. Don't do it again. Now, you have wasted two minutes of your valuable time. Be there at ten forty-five, no later."

After Warrior hung up, Lorne pressed the End Call button and turned to face her boss. "Get out. You'll have to find your own way back."

"I'm not leaving you, Lorne." Sean put his foot down.

"For God's sake, you *have* to. He's watching our every move. If he thinks I've gone back on my word, he'll kill them. Listen to me, Sean—we can still do this. Go back to the station, and I'll keep in touch with you."

Sean slammed on the brakes, unclasped his seatbelt, and threw open the driver's door, while Lorne clambered across the gearstick and settled behind the steering wheel.

"Stay safe, Lorne. Ring me at every opportunity you get, okay? Use your siren if you think time is against you."

"I will. But I need to keep the line open to him. There's no telling what will happen if I don't."

Sean withdrew his mobile from his jacket pocket and threw it onto the passenger seat. "Use that."

"All right. One last thing I want you to do for me, Sean."

His head tilted. "Which is?"

"When you get back to the station, ring Tony. Tell him I need his help."

"There's no need for that. We'll have your back, Lorne," Sean insisted.

"He's ex-MI6, Sean. It's his covert operational skills I'm thinking about. I better go. Just do it, please?"

He nodded then did something unexpected. He bent down and kissed her on the cheek. "Good luck."

Her cheeks warmed. She smiled, slammed the door shut, and sped away from him.

CHAPTER EIGHT

Sean returned to Regent Street and flagged down the nearest taxi to take him back to the station. He barged through the incident room doors, only to be bombarded by Katy's accusatory tone.

"Where is she? Did you get separated? Have you left her somewhere? Has the kidnapper got hold of her?"

"If you draw a breath for a second, I might be able to tell you, Sergeant." He flopped into the nearest available chair and watched AJ leave his seat to get him a cup of water from the dispenser. "Thanks, AJ. Jesus, what a morning."

"Christ, boss. Hurry up. Where's Lorne? Just tell us she's safe, will you?"

"Yes, she's safe. Warrior found out I was with her. Threatened that if I didn't jump ship the child would be hurt. We didn't have any choice but to do as instructed. I need to ring Tony."

"What? Why?" Katy perched her backside on the desk next to his.

"Lorne told me to. She wants him to follow her. It's a good idea, don't you think?"

"Actually, I do. Break the news to him gently. The last thing we want to do is upset either him or Charlie."

"I'm aware of that, Sergeant. Thank you." He took a sip of water and reached for the phone sitting on the desk. "I left my mobile with Lorne so we can contact her frequently."

"Glad to hear it. I'd hate the thought of leaving her alone and isolated out there," Katy sniped, crossing her arms and glaring at him.

"Okay, Katy, your annoyance is duly noted. If I can reiterate, it wasn't my decision to leave her out there on her *own*."

Katy nodded, and her eyes fluttered shut as if she were biting back another angry response.

He dialled Lorne's home number. "Hi, Charlie. Is Tony there please?"

"Who is this?" Charlie asked suspiciously.

"Sorry, love, I should have said. This is Sean, your mum's boss." He winced, knowing what was coming next.

"My God, is Mum okay?"

"She's fine. I just need a quick chat with Tony. She's asked me to have a word with him about something."

"Okay, he's outside mending a fence. I'll go and get him."

Sean tapped his fingers on the desk under Katy's intense gaze until Tony answered the phone.

"Sean? What's up?"

"Tony, I need you to get Charlie out of earshot first."

"Got it. Charlie, I might be a while. Can you go and pack my tools away, in case they get nicked?"

Sean could hear a chair being scraped across the floor, then Charlie said, "I'm not going anywhere. If this is about Mum, I have a right to know what's going on. We don't have secrets in this house. She'd be livid if you kept me out of the loop."

"Did you hear that, Sean?"

He blew out a breath. "I did. Stubborn girl, just like her damn mother. Okay, the news is neither good nor bad, Tony."

"Okay, let me sit down then. Hit me with it. I'm going to put you on speaker so Charlie can hear, okay?"

"Fine. You're both aware of the case Lorne is working on at the moment and what was going to take place today, yes?"

"Yep, the kidnapper was going to run her ragged, or so she thought. Has that changed?" Tony replied.

"No. Up until twenty minutes ago, I was with Lorne. Everything was going according to plan."

"*Was*? I'm not liking the sound of this, Sean. Where's my wife?"

"Tony, don't go off on one, mate. She's fine. The kidnapper must have eyes on her, in the form of an accomplice. They obviously reported back to this Warrior fella that I was with her. He rang Lorne and threatened to harm the baby if I didn't leave Lorne's side."

"Jesus! She's out there all alone—" Tony said.

"Oh no. Poor Mum, how could you let her down like that? I thought you were her friend, Sean?" Charlie's agonised voice pulled at his heartstrings.

He glanced up at Katy, who shrugged, then he ran a hand through his greying hair. "The decision wasn't mine to make, Charlie. Your mum urged me to go with clear instructions to ring Tony ASAP, hence the call."

"Why? Why did she tell you to ring us, apart from the obvious?" Tony asked.

"She wants you to follow her, Tony. You and Joe, in a covert operation. What do you say?"

"What do you think I'm going to say, man? Of course I will. It's a no-brainer."

Sean let out a relieved sigh. "Thank God for that. I'm still going to have to run this past the super first. I can't see her objecting, though she might insist on us calling in an Armed Response Team, too."

"Do that, Sean, and you will be seriously jeopardising the hostages' lives. We'll run things tightly between us. No risks, I swear. The kidnapper will continue to call the shots. The only thing in our favour is that Joe and I will be tracking Lorne's every move."

"That's reassuring in itself," Sean agreed.

"Wait! Won't that be putting Mum's life in extra danger?" Charlie asked.

"Your mum's life is always in danger, just being associated with the police. Think of it this way: she'll be under careful scrutiny from one of the best former agents around. That should put your mind at ease knowing that."

She exhaled noisily. "I suppose so. I'd rather her be in Tony's hands than yours at the end of the day, I guess."

Katy covered her mouth and sniggered at Sean's wide-eyed insulted expression. He cleared his throat. "Exactly. Of course Tony has the extra vested interest in being your mum's husband."

"Can we get back to the nitty-gritty details of the case?" Tony said.

"Okay. Her next rendezvous is about to take place soon. It's too late for you to get on her tail now. Let's hope he gives her a little more time in between rendezvous points so you and Joe can reach her. She has my mobile to keep us updated on her movements. Can you get on the road, and I'll contact you once she's rung me?"

"Okay, I'd suggest she rings me directly, but maybe we should keep things as they are. That way you can keep track of events should anything…"

"What? Go wrong?" Charlie said.

"I'm sure he didn't mean that, Charlie. Go awry, maybe. A tough challenge lies ahead of all of us, I suspect. We need to be vigilant at all times. Charlie, can you organise someone to be there with you? I know you'll snap my head off if I suggest you go under police protection," Sean said.

"I'll be careful. Carol will be here soon. I'll ask her to stay over for the next day or so. How's that?"

Sean bit the inside of his mouth and glanced up at Katy, who nodded her agreement. "Okay, any sign of trouble, and you ring the station ASAP. Got that?"

"Yes, Sean. I understand. Just bring Mum home safely. Promise me that."

"I promise, sweetheart. Give me your mobile number, Tony."

Tony reeled off the number, and Sean wrote it down. Then Tony announced, "I'm going to shoot off now. Keep in touch. I'll pick up Joe, and we'll head into the city centre. We can do this, bring *everyone* home safely."

Sean hung up and placed both hands over his face. "What a bloody mess. I better go and see the super."

He stood up, and as he passed Katy, she touched his arm and said, "She'll be fine. If anyone can bring this case to a swift and safe conclusion, it's Lorne."

"I know. I have no doubts about that, Katy. My apprehension lies with the kidnapper. He's obviously leading her into some kind of trap. I feel happier knowing that Tony is watching her back. With his skills, she'll be far safer than if I'd stuck with her; that's for sure. I'll be back soon."

Sean's footsteps grew heavier the closer he got to the super's office. He wondered how he would broach the subject of him deserting a vulnerable member of staff out in the field. He inhaled and exhaled before he entered the outer office then smiled when the super's secretary looked up at him.

"DCI Roberts, do you have an appointment?"

"No, it's an emergency. Does the super have a spare minute to see me?"

The older woman smiled and left her desk. She knocked on the super's door and walked in. Holding open the door, she announced Sean's arrival then stepped back to let him enter the room.

"Sorry, ma'am. It's an emergency."

The super nodded at the secretary to dismiss her and placed the pen she was using on the desk. "Sean? What kind of emergency? Everything all right at home, is it?"

"Yes, everything is fine there." His mouth twisted, and he chewed his lip a few times. "The case Lorne and I have been working this week has escalated out of our control." He filled her in on what had transpired and watched the changing expressions cross her face with interest.

"You left her out there, all alone? Did I hear that right?"

Sean tutted and held his hands, palms upwards, in front of him. "What was I supposed to do, ma'am?"

"If I were in your shoes, I'm not sure I would have done the same thing, but maybe that's the difference between us, Sean."

"What? Even when the child's life was threatened? Even Lorne urged me to leave. If she had any doubts, she wouldn't have told me to take a hike, would she?"

"We're going around in circles. What's done is done. You say Tony is agreeable to this? We've used him before on that truck job concerning Lorne's brother-in-law and that trafficker, haven't we?"

"Yes, there's no doubting Tony's ability to keep Lorne safe. The question is what this kidnapper has in store for her as his endgame."

"I can understand your apprehension; however, there is little we can do about that, given the circumstances. How is the case proceeding? What about the press conference? When is that scheduled for?"

"I've got Katy on that. Hopefully, it will take place today. I just wanted to bring you up to speed on things, ma'am, to keep you in the loop and to reassure you that Lorne is in the safest hands possible. Do we have your permission to proceed without getting an ART involved? I know it's going against procedure, but…"

"Yes, I'll take the flack if or when the shit starts flying, if things don't go according to plan."

Sean let out a relieved sigh. "Thank you, boss."

"Don't thank me, Chief Inspector. Just do your best to bring Lorne and the family home unharmed, okay?"

"Oh, yes, that is definitely my intention."

Anne White shuffled the papers on her desk and raised an eyebrow. "If that's all, Roberts, some of us have urgent paperwork to catch up on. Keep me informed, more frequently than you normally would on this one."

Sean rose from his chair and walked back towards the door. "Yes, ma'am."

Feeling considerably lighter on the return journey, his legs whisked him back to the incident room, which was ablaze with activity and a lot of shouting.

He clapped, bringing the team to attention. "Settle down, folks. Does someone want to tell me what's going on? Katy?"

Katy's eyes rolled up to the ceiling. "There's been another one, sir."

CHAPTER NINE

Lorne had a word with a taxi driver and persuaded him to let her park on the rank, she left the car and sprinted down Soho. She hated this part of town, and she shuddered at the thought of what went on behind closed doors in the shops surrounding her. Ordinary folk were under the illusion that the multitude of sex shops simply provided the general public with fun sex toys, but Lorne's stint with the vice squad around ten years ago had certainly opened her eyes to the true shenanigans that went on in this area of London. *No thanks! Neither Tony nor I need anything like this to keep our marriage fresh in the bedroom department. Makes you wonder if people's ways of thinking are getting weirder in this day and age. Probably not. Maybe it's me just getting older.*

She trotted past a few of the establishments with burly bouncers on the door, until she finally came to a halt outside the Happy Cock. Her mobile rang.

"Hello?"

"You're there, right?"

"Yes, as you well know."

"You can't get one over on me, Simpkins. You'd be wise not to bother trying from this point on. Do you hear me?"

"Yes. You've made yourself perfectly clear. What do you want me to do next?"

"Go inside. The girl behind the counter will have a surprise for you." Warrior sniggered like a teenage boy attempting his first kiss on a date.

Lorne cringed inside. *Shit! What bloody awaits me?* The call ended, and after inhaling a lungful of fresh air—well, as fresh as air gets in smoggy London—she entered the shop.

A pretty, leather-clad, petite woman smiled and beckoned her closer with a red-painted finger. "Come. My name is Anastasia. I show you good time, yes?" The girl sounded Eastern European, maybe Russian.

Lorne flashed her ID. "I think you've got the wrong impression, sweetheart. I'm not here for any kind of fun. The man on the phone said you would have something for me. What is it?"

"Come. You have to come back here. I show you." The girl pulled aside the luxurious aubergine-coloured curtain and motioned with her head for Lorne to follow her.

Lorne's insides clenched in spasms with trepidation. She placed her hands in her jacket pocket. In one, she found the clues she'd acquired so far—the key and the keyring—and in the other, she placed her hand over something that she hoped she wouldn't need to use to protect herself, her pepper spray. *God, I wish I'd had the foresight to arm myself with my Taser.*

"Come. Don't be scared... I no harm you. You enjoy the performance. I promise."

Lorne stopped short of going through to the back. When she reached the curtain, she strained her neck to see what lay beyond. A series of red glowing lamps lit a narrow passageway with numerous doors. *Jesus, the proverbial den of iniquity!* "I'd rather not. Just give me what Warrior wants me to pick up."

The woman laughed raucously until her mascara began to run down her heavily blushered cheeks. "You funny. You do as I say now, or the kid gets it."

Lorne glared at the woman. "And this sits well with you, does it? To hold a baby's life in your hands like that?"

The woman's laughter stopped, and a venomous look darkened her features. "Not me who has baby's fate in their hands. It's you. Now, do as I say."

The woman had changed from welcoming Lorne into her establishment with the promise of something pleasurable lying ahead to downright threatening her. Lorne relented but remained cautious as she agreed to go with the woman.

"No. Stop. I not stupid, lady cop. Empty your pockets on the counter."

Lorne tutted then did as she was told. "Here, that's it. I only have the clues your boss has supplied me with so far."

The woman patted Lorne's other pocket and shook her head in disgust. "You wait. I tell Warrior you try to deceive me. Give it me." She held her hand out, and Lorne ignored her hand and slammed the spray canister onto the glass counter.

"There. Satisfied?"

"No. I need to search for more. You destroy all trust now."

"I haven't got anything else. Lay one hand on me, and I'll break your bloody immaculately painted fingers in two. Am I making myself clear?"

Through narrowed eyes, the woman looked her up and down. "You nothing special, lady. I had boyfriend in KGB; he good at torture. You watch yourself, or you get sample of what he taught me."

Lorne shook her head. "You don't scare me. I've had my share of dealing with psychos over the years, and you're a pussycat in comparison. Shall we get on?"

"I'm in charge here. This my *gaff*, not yours. You take the orders. I *give* them."

"Whatever. Time's marching on," Lorne told her, tapping her foot in annoyance.

"Come with me. No funny business."

The smell of burning incense invaded Lorne's nostrils as she followed the woman up the hallway. At the end, the woman gave three short sharp taps on the door. Lorne prepared herself to strike.

A man of gigantic proportions pulled open the door. He had a goatee beard, and his huge muscles bulged beneath his taut shirt and waistcoat. "Is this her?" he asked the woman, leering at Lorne and giving her the once-over.

"Yeah. You have fun with her. She feisty, just the way you like them." The woman stepped backwards and rammed a hand in the centre of Lorne's back.

Lorne could do little to prevent herself surging forward into the giant's arms.

The woman and the man laughed. Lorne stared up at the man. The courage she always prided herself as having diminished quickly as his arms gripped hers, squeezing her muscles into painful submission.

"Please, don't hurt me." She despised herself for begging pitifully, but she had to say something. It felt as though the man's hands were crushing her bones.

He lifted her off her feet, swiftly moved across the floor, and threw her on the bed. The silky satin bedding softened the fall, but only a little. She stared up at the brute.

"Don't mess with me, bitch. Lie there and shut the fuck up."

Lorne gulped and nodded. She scooted back against the headboard and wrapped her arms around her knees, never once taking her eyes off the man. She'd only found herself in such a dire situation once before, and that was when the Unicorn had forced her into a hotel room years ago. The similarity between the two events caused her heart to pound faster. *I'm right! I have to be. He's got to be behind this. But how? He's dead.*

Two leather-clad girls entered the room and eyed her with interest. Lorne held firm, fighting the desire to bury her head in her hands.

"Get on with it," the giant ordered.

The girls promptly tottered on their high heels towards the bed. Barely inches away from Lorne, they began kissing. Their hands fondled and caressed each other's bodies. Lorne squeezed her eyes shut.

"Open them!" The man's booming voice filled the room, forcing her to watch the disgusting display.

She cringed as the girls started to undress each other, their tongues intertwining one second, lashing at each other's flesh the next.

Crap! Let me get out of here. She scanned the room using her peripheral vision, not wishing to alert the other occupants of her intention to attempt an escape. Nothing. The room was just that, a room. No windows. The only way out was the door she had come through. *Shit! I've had it.*

***

Warrior took the call from his boss while the baby was exercising his lungs.

"Can't you shut that thing up? I can't think straight, let alone hear what you're saying."

"They don't come with on/off switches. You want to be here when it really starts. I'm telling you, this is bloody minor."

"Right, I'll make this quick then. Are you ready?"

"Yep. All ready and good to go."

"Expect another delivery soon. And keep that copper on her toes. Don't let her stop and think for too long. She's more intelligent than you and me put together."

"She's enjoying herself at the moment in Soho."

Both men laughed.

"I don't want to know. I'm just glad things are going according to plan. Make sure you keep her team well out of reach, too."

"Yep, Max called in and said she'd dumped her DCI. She's now all alone out there."

"Don't take that for granted. Her car probably has some kind of tracking device on-board."

"Damn. Okay, good idea. I'll get her to dump it."

"Do what you have to do. Just keep her moving at all times. If nothing else, it'll mess with her brain. She's a thinker. Just remember that, and you'll do fine. I'm organising the endgame now. However, we have more plans to initiate before we get to the climax. I'm going to have fun with her when that finally comes around."

Warrior sniggered. "I can imagine."

"We'll up the pressure, make sure they take our request for that ten mill seriously. Mind you, when they hear about what's come to light today, they'll have no alternative but to take us seriously."

"Yes, boss."

His boss ended the call first. Tempted to harm him, Warrior glanced at the crying baby, but he had a feeling if he laid one hand on him, the decibels would sky-rocket into another universe. Instead, he went to fetch the child's mother. He crossed the yard to her hiding place then unlocked and lifted the doors. The woman shielded her eyes.

"Get out," he said, his voice bearing the signs of his frustration.

She held up her bound arms and waited for him to hoist her out of her prison dwelling, as usual. Without much effort, he deposited her beside him, her brow furrowed by unasked questions. "Come. The kid needs you. You have ten minutes to shut it up, or you'll both get hurt… and this time, I'm not messing about."

Her hands touched her face. "Babies don't work like that. He's used to me being around him twenty-four hours a day. Please, we need to be together. My husband will pay the money; have mercy on us. I promise I won't try to escape again or do anything foolish. You can keep me restrained. Just please, let me be with my child."

Her constant whining made his blood boil. He struck her with his fist, grabbed the rope around her wrists, and yanked her back into the house. "Cut the shit, lady, and deal with it. You've got exactly ten minutes, got that?"

The woman sobbed but tried to keep the noise to a minimum for her child's sake as she lifted him from his makeshift bed and rocked him back and forth to soothe his crying. Then she undid the button on her blouse and exposed her breast for the child to suckle, all under Warrior's close observation. He felt his crotch spring to life and began playing with his aching member. The woman quickly averted her eyes, much to his amusement.

"Have you ever been with a *real* man?" He laughed when he heard her swallow noisily. "Well?"

"My husband is a real man. He fathered my son. Isn't that what *real* men do? Not kidnap innocent women and children in the hope of getting money out of folks."

His laughter ceased. "I promise you, before you go back to him, I'll let you see what a real man can do for you, sweetheart."

The woman shuddered and held her baby tighter.

He looked at his watch and tapped the face. "Five minutes—actually, make it four. I've got things to do, and I need you shut away so I can do them without your constant pleading ringing in my ears."

She shot him a look laced with hatred. He grinned at her, revelling in the power he had asserted. When the time was up, she kissed the baby on the forehead and replaced him in the bag, speaking softly, urging him to go to sleep. He watched the touching scene with bile rising in his throat.

"Right, get going." He shoved her ahead of him, back outside to her cell, semi-admiring her compliance to do as instructed for a change. Maybe the suggestion about him showing her what a real man could do would serve to keep her in line. He watched her jump back into the hole then secured the doors again, before he made the call to Soho, and got on with his chores, while he awaited the new arrivals.

CHAPTER TEN

The girls had stripped down to their underwear and were in the process of lavishing intimate attention on each other and inching their way closer to Lorne. *Breathe! I mustn't let them see how scared I am.*

The thug eagerly watching the display unfolded his arms and withdrew his mobile from his pocket. He turned his back and answered it. Lorne strained her ear to hear the muffled conversation and, at the same time, tried to summon up the courage to bolt from the room. However, the man's call ended quickly. He clicked his fingers, and the girls instantly looked up at him.

"Enough," he ordered. "Playtime is over. This one has a mission to conclude."

The girls gathered their clothes and ran out of the room, leaving a bemused Lorne wondering what was about to happen to her next.

"Get up and come with me."

Lorne hesitantly followed the man out of the room and back into the shop, where the smiling assistant eyed her with curiosity.

"You enjoy, yes?" she asked, raising an inquisitive eyebrow.

Lorne shrugged a response. "Just give me the next clue and my new instructions."

"Give it to her," the unamused goon hissed.

The assistant gave her a wooden box. Lorne grabbed the rest of the clues and her pepper spray then rushed out of the shop, warily casting a watchful eye over her shoulder, in case her early release proved to be some kind of perverted trick. Outside, she let out the air she seemed to have been holding in for the past twenty minutes or so escape through her lips.

The box held instructions for her next destination, the London Eye, pod number fourteen, with a deadline of twelve noon. Lorne searched her immediate area, looking for a shop where something other than sex was on offer, like a food store of sorts, so she could grab something to eat whilst on the run. Finally, when she'd found her way back to the car, she spotted a small supermarket. She dipped into the shop, and her weary legs led her to the cold snacks area of a nearby fridge. She bought a tuna and mayo sandwich and a bottle of water then continued on her journey back to her car.

She pulled away from the taxi rank, opened the sandwich, took a bite, and searched for Sean's mobile phone. The phone in her office rang and rang until eventually, a breathless Katy answered it. "Jesus, I was just about to hang up. What took you so long?"

"We've got an emergency here, Lorne. Sorry."

She filtered into the main line of traffic. "What kind of emergency? Are you all right, Katy, is it the baby?"

"No. I'm fine. Another family has been kidnapped, Lorne. We have no way of knowing as yet if the crimes are connected, but that's what we're thinking right now."

"Shit. What the hell is going on? What's their intention, Katy?"

"We're at a loss to know that at this moment, Lorne. Leave us to deal with things at this end. What's going on there?"

"I'm on my way to the London Eye. Jesus, I don't really want to revisit the ordeal that they've just forced upon me. I'm shuddering just thinking about it."

"Are you all right? Did they hurt you?"

"Not physically, no. Mentally, though, I think I'll be scarred for life. I'm fine; ignore me. Any news on Tony? Did Sean contact him?"

"Of course. He's en route, picking Joe up on the way, awaiting further instructions from us."

"That's great. I feel safer already knowing that he'll be watching over me, even if it is from a distance. Things are quite tepid right now, but I fear they'll be intensifying as the day goes on. I'll check in later."

"Take care, Lorne. We've got you covered on this one. Be safe."

***

Katy ended the call and rushed back into the incident room. She marched over to the whiteboard and noted down Lorne's next destination before she re-joined the rest of the team.

"Everything all right? I take it that was Lorne," Sean asked, his forehead wrinkled with concern.

"Yeah, she's on her way to the London Eye. I'm going to ring Tony now, make him aware."

"No, I'll act as a go-between there. You concentrate on this case, Katy. I want to know how a family was abducted in broad daylight *again*."

"Okay, leave it with me."

Sean found a quiet corner amongst the hustle and bustle being generated by the rest of the team and contacted Tony. He returned and nodded at Katy. "It's done. He's not far from there now. It's a big relief to know that he and Joe have her within their sight, or they will have soon. What have we learnt so far on this new family?"

Katy shook her head. "To tell you the truth, not much. We have a female witness who has reported that she heard a woman scream. She turned to see what the commotion was about and saw a woman and a child, presumably the woman's daughter, being shoved into the back of a car in Chelsea."

"Where in Chelsea?"

"In an underground car park of a shopping centre," Katy replied.

"We need to get someone over there sharpish to question the woman and get as much information about the family abducted as possible."

"Do you want me to go?" Katy suggested.

"Might be a good idea. There's bound to be CCTV cameras in situ. Look through the footage, see what car she was either leaving or getting into or arrived in, and then we can see who we're dealing with and what impact that entails."

"Will do."

"As soon as we get that information, we can pay the relatives a visit. See if there's been any communication with the kidnappers."

"Yep, I'll leave Karen in charge of dealing with the conference, shall I?"

"Good idea. She can make the arrangements, but I'll be the one going in front of the camera. She's not experienced enough for that," Sean stated thoughtfully.

"She'd appreciate that. I'll get her to organise it right away. I don't think we should mention anything about this new case during the conference, agreed?"

"I agree. We need to keep quiet about it until all the facts are clear that we're dealing with the same kidnappers. How was Lorne? Did you tell her what was going on here?"

"Yeah, she seemed okay. Pleased that Tony will be within striking distance if she needs help. Perhaps she'll be able to get the info we need out of this Warrior chap, save us trying to link the dots between the two cases."

"If she can find a way of doing that, Lorne will do it. Her brain never shuts off," Sean said.

"Okay, I'll shoot off to the crime scene. Is it all right if AJ comes with me?"

"Of course. The rest of the team and I will get all the preliminary stuff started on the new case. Check in when you can."

Katy and AJ arrived at the multi-storey car park around fifteen minutes later. After assessing the scene for herself, Katy asked the attendant who was observing what was going on where she could view the CCTV footage. He showed her to a small room that acted as the eyes and ears of the car park. An elderly man was pressing buttons, working his way through the car park's many camera angles. *Excellent, this should be just what we need.*

She flashed her warrant card and introduced herself and AJ to the man. "Have you had a chance to search through the footage of the incident yet?"

"I have. I put it aside for you guys. Do you want me to set it up so you can see what happened?"

Katy smiled. "That would be brilliant."

The man pulled out a couple of collapsible stools from under the desk for Katy and AJ to sit on while their escort returned to the crime scene.

"I'm Ted, by the way. I used to be a copper years ago. So, what I did first was locate the crime on the tape, then I worked my way backwards. I hope my findings prove to be useful."

Katy glanced at AJ and raised an eyebrow then smiled at the man. "You're a star. Let's see what we have then, Ted."

He hit a button, and the incident played out on the monitor in front of them. "Here, the woman and her daughter were just about to get in her car when this black four-by-four screeched to a halt beside her. You can see how terrified she and her daughter were. It's as if they had an inkling what was about to take place."

"It must have been awful. Any chance you can get a close up on the number plates of both vehicles?"

"Let's see if we can get a clear picture for you; although, the woman's car is still at the crime scene. You can get the plate number from there."

"Great news. Do your best with the kidnapper's car, if you will."

The three of them sat in silence as the man fiddled with the camera angle and zoomed in and out until the image became clear. AJ gasped and cussed under his breath.

Katy sharply turned to look at him. "What? Do you recognise that plate, AJ?"

He swallowed and nodded. "Lorne was right. UNI 123 was associated with her arch enemy, the Unicorn."

"Jesus, really? It's his car? How can that be?" Katy asked, staring at the number on the screen.

"Okay, it's a few years ago now, but from what I can remember, the car actually belonged to Abromovski. I need to look back on the case file for clarification on that. He was up to his neck with Baldwin, aka the Unicorn. A lot of good it did him in the end. His demise came courtesy of Baldwin's own hands."

"Crap! What the hell is going on in that case? If Baldwin is dead and this Abromovski is dead, then how can this be happening? Ted, is it possible for you to give us a copy of the disc?"

The man picked up a CD case from the desk and handed it to Katy. "All ready for you. Listening to what you've just said, could this be one of the Unicorn's enemies, using the man's reputation to try and distract you?"

"Maybe, but then that doesn't really take into consideration the car, does it? Would one of his enemies be able to get his hands on it?"

AJ elbowed Katy gently. "I'm with Ted on this one, in a roundabout way. Number plates are easily copied. Slap it on a four-by-four, and you've got the police thinking they're dealing with an old enemy. I bet it's all a cover-up. Someone's toying with us. I'm willing to bet my pension on that."

Ted grunted. "I hope your pension is better than mine, lad. Why do you think I'm stuck in this tight office all day long?"

AJ smiled sympathetically at the man and squeezed his shoulder. "Hey, without your input, the case would be at a stalemate, Ted. We appreciate your help."

Katy shook the man's hand, and together, she and AJ walked back to the crime scene, where they noted down the number plate of the abducted woman's car. Then Katy spotted a young distraught-looking lady standing with a group of shoppers. She approached the woman and showed her ID. "Are you the person who reported the incident?"

"Yes. It was awful. I'd just parked my car, was sorting out the baby in the car seat when I heard this vehicle pull up, and the woman and child started screaming. I'm afraid I jumped back in my car. I feel guilty for not trying to help them…"

"Nonsense. No one would have expected you to have intervened. Your own baby's safety is paramount," Katy added, resisting the temptation to run a hand over her own little one growing inside.

Tears trickled down the woman's face. "Who would do such a thing? The woman was clinging to her teenage daughter, begging the men to let them go, but to no avail. The men dragged them by the hair and threw them into the back of their car."

"It must have been a terrifying ordeal. We're doing all we can to find these men. Can I ask if you heard any names mentioned perhaps?"

The woman thought the question over for a few seconds then shook her head. "I'm sorry, no. If they did use any, then I didn't catch it. I was in my car with the window wound up, though."

"Did anyone else see the incident?" Katy asked the rest of the crowd.

Everyone shook their heads, then a man offered, "We all appeared after the incident occurred. Most of us finished doing our shopping and found this young lady standing here, not knowing what to do. We just stuck around until you guys showed up to offer her some support."

"Thanks, that was kind of you," Katy told the man. Turning to speak to the woman again, she asked, "Would you mind giving us a statement?"

The idea appeared to panic the poor woman. "What? Now?"

"No. If it's easier, I can send a uniformed officer to take down the statement at your home later. I don't want to inconvenience you any more than necessary."

"Yes, that would be better. When my husband is home this evening, perhaps?"

"I can arrange that." AJ noted down the woman's address while Katy rang the station.

"Hi, boss. I have the woman's number plate. Can you get Karen or one of the lads to run it through the PNC for me?"

She heard Sean click his fingers to gain someone's attention. "Okay, shoot."

Katy gave the woman's details to Sean then sighed heavily.

"Everything all right, Katy?" Sean asked.

"Something else has cropped up. The attendant gave us the CCTV footage of the incident, and when I asked him to highlight the kidnapper's vehicle, the number plate UNI 123 came up."

"Is that significant, Sergeant?"

"AJ seems to think it has grave implications, yes. He wants to check through the previous case involving Baldwin, just to make sure. He recognised it as being connected to the Unicorn."

"Jesus, of course. It never dawned on me. I'll put out an alert on the vehicle at once. I'll also pull the file, see if he's right. Hang on. I've got a name and address for the latest victim. Maria Perkins, 24 Hilltop Rise, Fulham."

"Okay, we'll drop by the address now. Any news if she's married? If she is, where her hubby works? The likelihood is that we're dealing with another wealthy family. Could we be looking at another mega sum on their lives?"

"You head over there while we do some more digging here. I'll contact you with further information."

"Speak soon. Heading off now. By the way, can you get a PC to drop by Mrs. Caldecott's house this evening?"

"The lady who called in the incident? Sure."

Katy gave him the lady's address and hung up. She and AJ hopped back in the car and drove to the latest victim's address.

AJ let out a long whistle. "Looks like the kind of place where my folks would live."

"You mean a holiday home for your folks. I had to stifle a giggle back there when Ted was talking about his sucky pension. You won't be in the same boat of course."

He chuckled. "If I hadn't met you, I don't think it would have been long before Dad disinherited me."

Katy's eyes widened in shock. "Really? He would have gone to that extreme?"

AJ shrugged. "Who knows with my old man? When it comes to the crunch, all he really thinks about is his reputation."

"That's a bit harsh, love. He's always seemed nice to me."

Katy's mobile rang, interrupting their conversation. "Hello."

"Katy, it's Sean. I've got the info you need. The husband is another high-flyer in London, a Frank Perkins. His office is in central London. He's a technology bod."

"Okay, we're at the home address now, just pulled up, in fact. The place is all locked up. Electric security gates the lot. We'll head over to Mr. Perkins's office and be in touch soon."

Sean reeled off the address and hung up.

Katy let out a large sigh as AJ set off. "Crap, I'm beginning to feel some sympathy with Lorne here. All this flying around is a tad wearing."

"I wonder how she's getting on. Don't envy her in the slightest."

Katy and AJ parked in the underground car park and took the lift to the seventh floor. They flashed their IDs at the woman on reception, who rang the appropriate office and showed them to a door at the end of a narrow corridor.

"Mr. Perkins, I'm Detective Sergeant Katy Foster, and this is my partner, DS Alan Jackson."

He stood, shook their hands, and invited them to take a seat. "What's this concerning, Sergeant?"

"I take it your surprise to see us means that no one has made contact with you as yet."

The man reclined in his chair, wearing a frown. "I'm not with you. Why would someone be contacting me on police business? To my knowledge, I haven't done anything unlawful."

"It's nothing to do with your business, per se. It is with deep regret, I need to inform you that we have reason to believe your wife and child were abducted a few hours ago."

The man's face clouded over, and he catapulted forward in his chair. "What? Where? When? Why?" Agitated, he swept a hand over his face.

"We believe your wife might have been on a shopping trip with your daughter. Is that right?"

"My wife said she was taking my daughter to the dentist. There's every chance she might have gone shopping afterwards, yes. Oh, Lord, why?"

"That we don't know until the kidnappers make contact. We're dealing with a similar case right now, which could be connected. I have to ask if you know a Lance Hardy?"

"Yes, he's a good friend of mine. I don't understand. Does he have something to do with my wife's abduction? Is that what you're telling me, Sergeant?"

"No, sorry to mislead you. Mr. Hardy's wife and child have also been kidnapped."

"Bloody hell. When?"

"Yesterday, we believe. We have experienced officers out in the field, trying to track down the abductors now."

"What do these bastards want? Have they said? Why haven't they rung me?"

"We're still trying to get to grips with the case, Mr. Perkins. They're demanding a large sum of money from Mr. Hardy. We're presuming the same thing is going to happen with you."

"Crap. So what do we do until then? Just sit and wait for the call?"

"Yes, there's very little we can do. We've put out an alert for the car, in the hope we might learn which direction the kidnappers took after the abduction. At this time, that's all we can do."

The intercom on his desk tinkled to life. "What is it, Susan?"

"There's a strange call for you, sir. The caller insisted it was a matter of life or death that he speaks to you at once."

"Then put him through."

The phone rang, and Perkins reached for it.

"Can you answer it on speaker phone so we all hear?"

Perkins nodded.

Then Katy advised, "Try and remain calm at all times. There's every possibility he will set out to goad you. Just restrain yourself from reacting, for your family's sake."

"Hello. How can I help you?" Perkins answered the call, forcing brightness into his voice.

"We've got your wife and kid. Our demands are that we're giving you twenty-four hours to come up with ten million."

"What? But I don't have that sum of money lying around." Perkins's mouth ran away from him before his brain had the chance to engage.

"Not my problem. You either want to see your family again, or you don't. The choice is yours. Their lives are in your hands. I have a feeling you'll do what's necessary to get them returned to you in one piece and unharmed, *won't you?*"

Katy urged Perkins to agree with the kidnapper.

"Yes, of course. I'll do what I have to do to bring my family home. Just tell me what to do."

"I just have. Get the money together and await further orders."

"Can I have proof that my family are okay?" Perkins asked, pulling a face at Katy as if doubting he'd said the right thing.

She approved of his question and gave him the thumbs-up.

"Next time. They're indisposed at present." The man's laughter filled the room.

"Don't hurt them, please. I'll get you the money; I promise."

"Thought that might make you see sense. I'll be in touch soon."

The man hung up, and Perkins pressed the button on the phone, silencing the dial tone. His hand swept through his hair. "My God, where am I supposed to lay my hands on that sort of money? Does this man understand what a dismal financial climate we're entrenched in right now? Does Lance have the funds to honour their demands?"

Katy nodded. "That's our understanding, yes. What about the bank? Will they give you a loan?"

"Of ten million? Are you mad? Sorry, no offence, but Christ, I went to them cap in hand only last month for five hundred grand, and they laughed at me." He shook his head in despair. "Twenty-four hours to get my hands on that kind of money—that's simply impossible."

"You need to try. I'm sorry; I'm just stating the facts. What about family members? Can they help out with a personal loan maybe?"

"No. I'm the only one in our family with any hint of wealth. If only I hadn't invested heavily in the stock market before it collapsed. Please, Sergeant, I need my family back, unharmed if that's at all possible. They're the air that I breathe. I'll be totally lost without them." He glanced sideways at the framed photo of his wife and daughter sitting next to the phone on his desk.

"I understand. We're doing our best to track these kidnappers down. However, they're not making it easy for us. Can you think of anyone, either businesswise or personally, who is carrying a huge grudge that would drive them to do this to you? Is there a transaction you've made recently that could have pissed someone off?"

"No, nothing. Business has been slow for weeks, months even. What about Lance? Could he suggest a culprit?"

"He had an inkling, which we followed up on, only to receive a negative result."

"So, where do we go from here?"

"We're going back to the station now, to continue our investigation, and I'd advise you ringing around associates, friends, and other banks to try and find the funds to satisfy the greed of the kidnappers." Katy handed him a card, then she and AJ rose from their seats and shook Perkins's hand.

"That's it? You're ostensibly telling me to stomp up the money and deal with it?" His anger suddenly emerged and caused his voice to tremble.

"I'm sorry. That's the way it has to be. Gone are the days when the Met can come up with the cash in an instant to bail families out. We're under strict financial constraints, too, unfortunately."

He inhaled a long breath and shrugged. "I apologise for my outburst."

"There's no need. We'll stay in touch, Mr. Perkins. Please bear in mind we have extremely experienced officers working on both cases, yours and Mr. Hardy's."

"Thank you. I'll ring you if I manage to lay my hands on the money."

CHAPTER ELEVEN

During the course of the drive and totally fed-up with travelling back and forth on the same roads, Lorne bolted down her sandwich, unsure when or where her next meal would pass her lips. She regretted her actions soon after when some of her lunch refused to settle in her stomach and lodged itself in her windpipe. She pulled into the car park and twisted the cap off the bottle of water. She took a gulp, trying to shift the tenacious lump in the throat.

Soon after she went in search of pod fourteen of the London Eye. She had visited the tourist attraction on numerous occasions with either Charlie or her father. However, she sensed this expedition might hamper any enjoyment of returning in the future.

"Hello, madame. Just the one ticket, is it?"

Lorne nodded and handed over her credit card, hopeful the Met would reimburse her later. "Thanks." She leaned in and told the man in the ticket office, "I'm with the Met police, working a huge sensitive case at the moment."

He raised an eyebrow as if he thought she was pulling a fast one to avoid paying. "Okay."

"No, seriously, I am." She showed him her warrant card, and that appeared to appease him. "I've been given clear instructions to get a ride on pod fourteen. Can you arrange that for me?"

The man cast his gaze up to the ride. "That pod isn't going to be available for at least fifteen minutes. Will that suit you?"

Lorne hitched up her right shoulder and tutted. "It'll have to be okay."

The man issued her a ticket and pointed out where she should stand next. Once she had joined the queue, Lorne pretended to be reading one of the ride's brochures she had picked up during her conversation and sneakily began looking around her. Her suspicions were drawn to anyone in the milling crowd who glanced her way as if they were watching her. Then her heart started to race. For the briefest of seconds, she saw a wisp of black, a man's jacket disappear behind a nearby wooden hut. Her eyes remained trained to that spot for the next five minutes, but when nobody reappeared, she put the incident down to her overactive imagination and tired eyes playing a trick on her.

Finally, the attendant gave her the go-ahead to climb aboard the recently vacated pod. She was amongst ten other passengers, mostly

Japanese tourists, who shuffled into the capsule. As the oversized Ferris wheel began its agonisingly slow journey, Lorne moved to the front of the pod, and her gaze sought out the hut that had held her interest moments before. A relieved smile touched her lips when she recognised the figures of her husband and his colleague, Joe. *Thank God, I'll be safe with them both close by.*

Thoughts of being at home with Charlie and Tony, enjoying one of their renowned family barbecues, were quickly brushed aside, however, when her mobile rang. "Hello."

"You made it then, Simpkins. By the end of this trip, I want you to note down five locations in your eye-line which are visited daily by at least a thousand people."

"What? Is this some kind of joke? What does that have to do with releasing the family?"

"Are you questioning me, again?"

"No. Sorry, I don't mean to, but come on—"

"And FYI, you now have *two* families on your conscience, Mrs. Super Copper Extraordinaire."

He hung up, leaving her feeling frustrated. She took out the notebook and pen she always carried in her jacket pocket and began scribbling down the tourist locations he'd hinted at. She didn't really need to have the sites in her eye-line—she was a Londoner born and bred, and that came with an inbuilt knowledge of places to avoid in the peak season. When she had completed her task, she revisited her conversation with Katy about the new family and a possible connection. She nodded to herself. *So he's upped the ante. But will he stop at two families?*

She withdrew Sean's phone from her pocket and dialled the incident room.

Sean picked up after only two rings. "Are you all right, Lorne?"

"I'm fine. Look, I'm just checking in. He's given me a mind-numbing task to keep me amused during my trip. I'm guessing he'll ring back once his cohort informs him that I'm nearing the end of my trip. He's just admitted that they're holding two families hostage now, so I wanted to tell Katy that she was right in her line of thinking."

"That's good to know. She's just rung. I'm expecting her back any moment. Any sign of Tony and Joe yet?"

"Yeah, I've spotted them. I just hope my tail hasn't got wind of them being close by. Any news on the press conference yet? Airing that is either going to blow these cases wide open or cause irreparable damage."

"I agree. It's all in hand. Scheduled to go out live in a few hours. Don't laugh, but I've volunteered to go before the cameras."

Lorne laughed in spite of his warning. "Sorry. Ugh… are you all right with that?"

"My stomach is somersaulting itself into knots right now. If Katy comes back in time, I might try and persuade her to do it instead."

"If she's not feeling sick, then I would definitely encourage her to take up the reins of that one." Lorne covered the mouthpiece with her cupped hand and whispered, "What about the money side of things? Can either of the families afford to meet the gang's ransom demands?"

"Hardy is begging and borrowing as we speak, but Katy doesn't hold out much hope of Perkins coming up with the money."

"Can the Met help out at all, Sean?"

"Once upon a time, I would have said yes without hesitation, but you know as well as I do how much the budget cuts have affected the force."

"Do me a favour, ask the super? See if we can bend the rules slightly on this one or at least find part of what is expected."

"That's all very well asking that, Lorne, but what happens if the kidnappers abduct yet another family and then another? What are we supposed to do then?"

"Please ask Anne just this once, for me?"

"Like I have a choice!" he grumbled.

She blew him a kiss down the line. He responded by ending the call. She could feel her cheeks warm as she took in the amazing view once more. The anxieties of the day subsided during the ride but materialised once more when Warrior made contact with her again near the end of the pod's cycle.

"Got them, Simpkins?"

"Yes. You want me to tell you the locations now?"

"Just one."

Lorne frowned. Not knowing in which direction the conversation was going in annoyed her. "The Victoria and Albert Museum. How's that? Do I win?"

"Cut the shit, wise mouth. That's going to be your next destination." He paused for a moment then issued her the obligatory time limit as if he were working out the route and how long it would take her to get there. "You've got an hour from the time you get off the pod. Got that?"

"Jesus! I'll never make it."

"I can't hear you! Lame excuses don't wash with me, lady. Get your effing arse into gear and move it."

Lorne placed her mobile in her jacket pocket as the pod shuddered to a halt. She apologised to the other tourists as she brushed past them to get out of the door first. She ran back to the car and started the engine then fished out Sean's mobile and rang the station again. "I'm en route to the V&A. Can't chat; I'm against a stiff time limit. Let Tony know." She hung up without giving Sean the chance to reply.

***

Warrior was fully prepared for the new arrivals when Johnny and Spike unloaded the petrified woman and her child from the car. "Any trouble?"

"Not really. They tried to resist, but a few well-placed slaps seemed to do the trick in keeping them quiet," Johnny informed him with a laugh.

"Shit happens, eh? The boss said not to touch them. But then he's not the one having to deal with the bollocks they're dishing out, is he?" Warrior said.

The two goons grumbled their agreement, and each grabbed one of the hostages by the arm and guided them roughly towards the back door of the house. The teenager had other ideas, though, and when the opportunity opened up, she slipped out of her guard's grasp and ran across the yard, screaming. She didn't get very far, though, before her guard recaptured her and hauled her back to stand alongside her mother.

Warrior glared at the child, slapped her face hard, and warned them both, "Any more shit like that, and someone is going to get seriously hurt. Am I making myself clear?"

The tearful mother reached for her daughter's hand and squeezed it. "I promise, neither Kerry nor I will give you any more trouble. Please, don't harm us."

Warrior moved to within five inches of the girl's face. "Keep her in line, and that might just happen. Got that, Kerry?" The teenager held her head down and angled it away from him. He grabbed her chin and forced her to look him in the eye. "Answer me, or I'll set the boys on you, and believe me, they can be savages once I give them the green light."

"I understand. I'm sorry." The girl's quivering voice came out as an apologetic whisper.

Warrior relinquished his grip and led the party into the house. He stopped halfway along the dimly lit hallway and opened a cupboard door under the stairs. Johnny pushed the mother towards him, and Warrior ordered her to get into the cupboard. The woman sensibly did so without causing any hassle. Warrior had a feeling that wouldn't be the case with the feisty teenager, so once he'd shut the door on the mother, he withdraw a length of rope from his pocket and wrapped it around the girl's wrists while the other two men held her tightly. "Just in case you think about going back on your word."

"I won't. Ouch… that's hurting me," she cried out.

Warrior's eyes narrowed. "Shut up, bitch." He opened a smaller door and thrust the girl inside the dark area then slammed the door on her noisy objections. "Hey, Momma, you better have another word with your daughter when we're gone. I don't think she's quite got the message yet. If I return in thirty minutes and hear her utter one single word, I will have no hesitation in following through on my threat. Is that clear?"

"Yes, I'll talk to her," the mother's distant, shaking voice replied.

Warrior and his two associates walked back into the kitchen and were immediately confronted by the crying baby. "Jesus! This is bloody never ending. Now the damn kid is hungry."

Johnny sniggered. "How do you know that? It could have just shat its nappy."

"Don't ask. I think by the time we get out of here, I'll be some kind of bloody expert on babies." He shuddered. "The thought appals me. Why do people have 'em? Especially when there's the possibility of them turning out to be like you guys!" Warrior laughed at the offended looks on the other men's faces. "Johnny, go and get the other woman. You guys can get a thrill out of her feeding the kid."

"Yuck, using her tits?" Johnny replied before he left the house. He returned with Bethany, who looked tired and fearful.

"The kid needs you. The boys have volunteered to keep an eye on you while I get a break from the kid's crying."

Her head swivelled between the three men. "That's not fair. I need some privacy while I feed my son."

He raised a questioning eyebrow. "Are you refusing to shut the kid up?"

"No, I want to feed my son. I just don't think it's right that you expect me to perform in front of an ogling audience. I beg of you, don't put me through such an ordeal."

"I don't get you women. I hear and see it all the time on TV, how you think feeding a kid is the most natural thing in the world, and now you're telling me you're refusing to do it?"

"It is, and I'm not refusing... please, don't ask me to do it in front of you as if you're treating it like a perverted game."

Warrior flung his arm in the air. "I give up. Boys, do what you want with her, and if the kid continues to cry because of her refusal to feed him, then kill it."

Bethany flung herself on the floor at his feet. "No! I didn't mean to..." He kicked her away and marched out of the house without looking back.

Even his hardened heart skipped a beat when her continuous screams filled the surrounding area. *These women have to learn who's boss.* He walked away from the house, the screams becoming less and less the farther he ambled along the overgrown track that led to the house. He picked up a small rock and lobbed it over the stone wall at an inquisitive crow watching him. "Get out of here, you little bastard! Come back later. When we're finished, there'll be a corpse or two for you and your mates to have a feast on." He laughed at his cruel joke then slowly made his way back up the track to the farmhouse.

CHAPTER TWELVE

Lorne glanced anxiously at her watch. She'd been standing outside the Victoria and Albert Museum for about five minutes, awaiting further instructions. She checked her phone to see if the battery had possibly run out—it hadn't. *Where are you? Ring me, damn it!* Her people-observation skills had certainly intensified during the morning's venture, but not well enough for her to figure out who Warrior's accomplice was in the crowd meandering around her. She hadn't managed to get a visual on Tony at the location, either, and that only added to her frustrations. Her mobile jingled, and she scrambled to answer it. "Hello."

"You made it then. I'm late, I know; I got tied up here. New deliveries, people not doing as they're told, dishing out punishments—it all takes time to sort out, as you can appreciate."

"What? Please tell me you haven't hurt anyone?"

"Why ask when I've just told you that I've been dishing out punishments. Are you deaf now?"

"No. Sorry. Please, there's no need for you to hurt the hostages. I'm doing everything you ask of me."

"*You* might be, but if they start playing up at this end, I'll ensure they regret their dumb actions. Now, enough of that. Where's next on your agenda?"

Lorne frowned. "What? I don't understand. You haven't told me what clue I should be looking for."

"No clue here. And *stop* questioning my orders."

Lorne's eyes fluttered shut. "I apologise; it wasn't intentional."

"Next?" he repeated sharply.

She opened her eyes and picked out another famous landmark from her list. "Umm… St. Paul's Cathedral was the next location I jotted down."

"Then what are you waiting for? Off you go. Let's see…" He paused for a moment then added, "I'll be generous and give you an hour and twenty minutes this time." He hung up.

Lorne trotted back to the car, which she'd parked illegally on double yellow lines, only to find an enthusiastic traffic warden in the process of writing her another damn ticket. *Crap! Not again. No wonder the bloody tourists always complain about London's over-zealous wardens.* She flashed her warrant card as she opened the driver's door. "Sorry, I'm on an important case. It's a matter of life and death. I don't have time to hang around."

The warden glowered at her, quickly signed and tore off the ticket, then tucked it in the plastic wallet and slapped it on the windscreen before she had the chance to pull away. *You officious shithead.* She sped away, looked back in the mirror at the grinning warden, and gave him the finger. He tipped his cap at her and raised his thumb in response.

Lorne again reported her destination to Sean back at the station.

"Christ, he's really giving you the run-around. Stick with it, Lorne, not that you have any other options."

"He mentioned something disconcerting. Told me that he'd handed out some form of punishment to the hostages, wouldn't give me any indication as to what form that had taken, though."

"Damn. Not what we wanted to hear. Quick update for you; I know time is precious. Katy's just about to go before the cameras now. She has Hardy sitting in on the conference, too. No news on the money from either party as yet. Time's marching on, and the two husbands are beginning to get worried."

"That's understandable. Don't, for goodness sake, let them know that their families might have suffered, will you? Look, I need to concentrate on my driving. I didn't spot Tony at the last location. I take it he was there with me."

"As far as I know. I'll get in touch with him now. Want me to ask him to get your attention at St. Paul's?"

"Yep, just for peace of mind. Thanks, Sean. Wish Katy good luck from me. Let's hope one of the viewers can give us a heads-up on the cars and where their likely destination is. I have a feeling these guys are well-organised and have allowed for a few screw-ups along the way."

"Sounds about right. Just remain alert at all times and don't forget Tony and Joe will be within a few feet of you if you run into trouble again."

"Yep. Speak soon."

Lorne disconnected the call then tapped her fingers as the traffic ahead of her moved in quick bursts. When it ground to a halt at some roadworks, she seized the opportunity to ring home to check on Charlie.

"God, I've been worried sick about you, Mum."

"There's no need, love. Tony's following me. How are things there? All right?"

"Yeah. Carol and I were just about to have some lunch. Have you eaten? You need to keep your strength up."

Lorne laughed. "Yes, dear. I gulped down a sandwich a while back. Can you put Carol on?"

"Hello, Lorne." Carol's calming voice came on the line.

"Hi, Carol. No news from me, except this guy is sending me here, there, and everywhere with no real end in sight. I don't suppose you've picked up on anything, have you?"

"Not really, Lorne. The spirits are warning you to stay alert at all times. You'll be doing that anyway, right? Stay focused. I feel encouraged that everything will turn out for the best, knowing that Tony is following you."

"Don't worry about me. Stay safe there, both of you, okay?"

"We will, love. I'll stay overnight to keep Charlie company. Be safe, Lorne. Let Pete and your father be your guiding light and source of protection."

"Love you both," Lorne said then hung up. She wiped away a tear that had dripped onto her face. She was heartened to hear that Pete and her father were watching over her, keeping her safe. She just hoped that was all it was and that they weren't gathering to help her make the transition to the afterlife.

***

Katy felt surprisingly anxious as she sat in front of the cameras. She didn't usually have a problem talking to the media. *Why this time?* Maybe it was because she'd never really been involved in a high-profile kidnapping case before. She turned to Mr. Hardy and smiled. "How are you coping?"

"To put it bluntly, I'm not."

The reply raised her anxiety levels to their limit. She inhaled and exhaled a few calming breaths.

The cameras rolled, and Katy's nerves subsided as she reeled off the information regarding the Orion car stolen from Mrs. Jenkins, the Hardys' neighbour, and gave the go- ahead for the reporters present to start firing their questions.

"What was behind the attack? Do you know, Sergeant?" asked a young blonde reporter sitting at the front of the crowd.

"We believe the car was used as a getaway vehicle. Unfortunately, Mr. Hardy's wife and child were abducted from their home on the same day. If anyone recognises the vehicle or its number plate—it must be out there somewhere—please contact us immediately. Saying that, there is every chance that this violent man struck again and replaced the Orion with yet another vehicle. Has your vehicle been stolen in the London area this week? I appreciate it's a vast area, but we're willing to follow up on any leads that come our way right now. Our aim is to get this family reunited as soon as possible. An infant is at risk here."

An older journalist raised his hand, and Katy nodded for him to speak. "You say a child and mother have been abducted. Does that infer we're talking about a kidnapping case here, Sergeant? It seems a little strange the police calling a press conference just about a stolen car."

"Yes. I'm sorry to have misled you slightly. That's our main objective here. I wanted to get this lady's stolen vehicle placed firmly in the minds of the viewers before I led onto the main aspect of this crime. It's imperative we locate the vehicle first and foremost."

"I see. It just sounded strange for you not to mention the mother and child as your priority," the same journalist suggested, smiling smugly at her.

Katy could feel her cheeks warming up. She turned to look at Mr. Hardy, who was staring back at her with a concerned frown furrowing his brow. Katy faced the crowd of eager journalists and responded to the allegation calmly, with, she hoped, more confidence than she felt. "As I have stated already, it was my intention to focus on the vehicle first. Unfortunately, we have no clear indication why Mr. Hardy's family are being held hostage."

The same smug journalist asked yet another question: "Is there a ransom involved? That's usually a good indication of why a family is being held hostage, Sergeant."

Katy seethed but refused to show how much the infuriating journalist was getting under her skin. She looked him directly in the eye and replied, "Yes, there has been a ransom demand made."

He tilted his head slightly and tapped his pen against his chin before he continued. "Surely, by going in front of the cameras, are you not putting this family's life in jeopardy? Don't kidnappers usually threaten that if the family goes to the police, they'll hurt the hostages—or even worse, kill them?"

"Usually, that is the case. However, in this instance, the kidnappers haven't told us that. Do you really think I would be holding this conference if we'd been warned about that?"

"Just asking the question, Sergeant."

Katy nodded at him. "Any more questions?" She wanted to add the words *dumb* or *otherwise* to her question, but she restrained herself.

The crowd fired off a few more insignificant questions, which Katy duly answered before she handed the stage over to Mr. Hardy to issue a plea for his wife and son's safety. Soon after, the crowd dispersed, and Katy led Mr. Hardy out to his car.

Katy shook his hand and watched him get in his vehicle. "I'm sorry about that," she said, resting her elbow on the top of his open door.

"There's no need, Sergeant. I understand completely the angle you were working on. Do you think that journalist was right?"

"About what?"

"Could we have just put my family's life in more jeopardy by doing the conference?"

"To be honest with you, we have no way of knowing. However, I very much doubt it. I'll be in touch soon. Stay strong."

Katy remained where she was for a few seconds after Mr. Hardy's car had left the car park, mostly to gather her thoughts on how to proceed next. Out of the corner of her eye, she saw the smug journalist approaching her, and she intentionally set off in the opposite direction before he could barrage her with more unanswerable questions. She expected him to call out some kind of jibe, but he didn't. She walked around the block then re-entered the building and ascended the stairs to the incident room.

AJ glanced her way. "Are you all right?"

"Yeah, I just needed a bit of fresh air. Anything come in yet?"

"One or two sightings we need to chase up on. I'm pretty positive about them."

Her spirits instantly lifted. "Fabulous news. I'll check in with the boss and get back to you." She walked into her old office and found the chief sitting at the desk, looking contemplative. "Have you heard from Lorne, boss?"

"Yes. She's on her way to St. Paul's now."

"Is Tony with her?"

"He is. Close behind her, anyway."

"Then what's wrong?"

He shrugged. "I can't really put my finger on it, Katy. Something just doesn't feel right."

Katy plonked down in the chair and sighed. "In what way?"

"That's all I can tell you at present. Never mind my ludicrous feelings of doubt. How did the conference go?"

"It went."

"Eek... that bad, eh?"

"One bolshie journalist out of twenty isn't so bad, I suppose. The good news is AJ has just informed me that we've got a few sightings of the stolen vehicle to chase up."

"That's brilliant. Do you want to do that with AJ this afternoon? Have you eaten lunch yet?"

"No, not sure if I could keep anything down. My stomach is still in knots about the conference."

"You should have said. I would have taken over if I'd known it was going to upset you that much."

"I have to get on with things, Sean. I can't let the baby stand in the way of me conducting my job properly all the time."

"Well, I'm going to send one of the lads out to pick up some pizzas. How's that?"

"Sounds like a greasy nightmare that's sure to make me feel queasy for the rest of the day," Katy said.

"I'll get them to rustle up a salad for you. No dressing, in that case."

"You do that. I'm going to crack on with the team, see how things are progressing. Any news from Perkins on whether he'll be able to come up with the money or not?"

"No, nothing. Last I heard, he wasn't holding out much hope. I'll give him a ring after I've placed the lunch order."

Katy rose and threw over her shoulder as she walked towards the door, "Nice to see you have your priorities in order there, boss."

She closed the door just in time, before the missile he launched hit the door.

CHAPTER THIRTEEN

Warrior and his men were watching the conference together in the kitchen of the farmhouse on an old portable TV. About halfway through the transmission, Warrior received a call from his boss.

"Yes, boss."

"Are you watching this?" The man's thick Eastern European accent was highlighted as he vented his anger.

"We are. What do you want us to do about it?"

"You're a bloody idiot. Did you not warn that Simpkins woman what the consequences would be if the case appeared on the news?"

"Er…"

His boss cursed in his own language for several seconds then went quiet.

"Are you still there?" Warrior asked hesitantly.

"I'm here. Leave me to think a moment. Right, the plan has just altered."

"In what way?" Warrior asked, dreading what direction his next instructions would be taking. His boss always expected the impossible when things didn't go according to plan.

"Our plans need to be brought forward. Ring the Hardy man, make him aware of the damage he has caused and the fact that his wife and child's lives are hanging by a thread because of his stupidity. Tell him he only has until seven this evening to produce the money, or they will both be killed."

"But, boss, killing his family wasn't part of the plan."

The other two men listening in on his side of the conversation stared nonplussed at him and shook their heads.

"I'm not sure my boys are up to that."

"Well, if they're not up to the task, then I'll get a team in who is. What did they expect would happen when they signed up for this job? To sit around playing board games all the time?"

"No, boss. I'll try and persuade them."

"No *try* about it, man—you'll do *it*, or none of you will get paid. Am I making myself clear here? I know English isn't my native tongue, so I want to make sure you comprehend what is at stake if either of you refuse to go ahead with the new arrangements."

"There's no need to spell it out, boss. The lads understand and will do as instructed should the money not appear by seven."

"Okay, until that time, I want your men to go out and pick up the third family. Let's keep them on their toes at all times."

Warrior swallowed hard. "Christ, I didn't think we would get to that point. I'll need to make room for them here first."

His boss grunted. "Not my problem. I told you to be ready for every eventuality. Now get on it. And stop being so nice to that copper. Bombard her with impossible tasks and ensure she knows she has the families' lives, all three of them, in her hands. Heap the pressure on at every opportunity."

"Yes, boss. Leave it with me."

"If you find you're out of your depth, let me know, and I'll get a replacement to run things."

"There's no need. We're all focused on what needs to take place and the time limits you've set. I'll ring the copper now."

"You do that. Stop pandering to her and start getting tough. You hear me?"

"On it now, boss."

Once his boss hung up, Warrior tore around the room like a tornado. When he'd calmed down and got his head around what needed to take place next, he stood in front of his men and glared at them. "Right, either we do as he says, or we don't get paid. It's as simple as that."

"We've done that already, mate. I didn't sign up to kill people. That don't sit right with me, dammit," Johnny whined.

Warrior jabbed his thumb at an area over his shoulder. "There's the door, mate. The choice is yours."

Johnny heaved a reluctant sigh. "All right. What do we do next?"

Warrior paced the floor and ran his hands through his cropped hair. "You two need to get back out there and snatch the next family. I'll do the necessary around here in the meantime. Now get out of my hair and don't come back empty-handed."

Both men nodded then rushed out of the house. Warrior heard the screech of the car departing before he rang Lorne.

"Your lot have screwed up, Simpkins. Big time."

"What? I don't understand. What's happened?"

"Don't act all innocent with me. Things have changed dramatically because of their fuck-up. So listen carefully, or the Hardys' lives will be ended before the sun sets this evening."

"What? You can't do that—we had a deal."

"Fuck off giving me objections and frigging listen. You ring your mates and let them know Hardy has until seven this evening to come up with the dosh—not half of it, either. I want the full ten mill or else his family will be killed and buried in a secret location. He'll never find out if they're dead or alive. A waste, I know, but that's what the boss wants."

"Okay, I'll pass the message on. I'm close to St. Paul's now. What do you want me to do next?"

"For a start, you can shut your mouth and listen for a change. If you think you've been run off your feet up until now, you'd be disillusioned by that assumption. I'll have further instructions for you shortly."

***

Lorne didn't know what part of her was spinning more—her insides or her head. She hated feeling useless and totally out of control of a situation. She picked up Sean's mobile and spoke to him on speakerphone as she continued to weave her way through the agonisingly slow traffic.

"Sean, I haven't got long. They didn't like it."

"Like what, Lorne?"

"The conference. We've stuffed up. You have to pass on a message to Hardy that he's got until seven tonight to raise the funds or his family will be killed."

"I hear you on that. What about the Perkins? Did he mention how they fared?"

"No. He didn't say. I'd prepare Mr. Perkins for the same kind of fate and urge him to pull out all the stops. Who knows what's going to happen once the seven o'clock deadline passes."

"Shit! Okay, how are you holding up, Lorne?"

"I'm okay. Weary, but I have to keep going. He's also told me that my involvement is going to be escalated, too."

"Meaning what?"

"I have no idea. I get the feeling they're giving me the run-around just to keep me occupied and away from the station."

"So you've changed your mind on the Unicorn's connection then?"

"I'm really not sure, Sean. I'm depending on you guys not to let me down back there. Throw everything you've got into finding that vehicle—both vehicles, in fact. Someone knows where they are. That's going to be the key to this now."

"Okay. We'll up the tempo at this end. I'll get on to Hardy and Perkins first then help the team sift through any calls that come in from the conference. Stay safe. Don't drop your guard at all. You hear me?"

"That goes without saying. Call you later."

She peered into her rear-view mirror, looking for Tony and Joe. She spotted them three cars back and let out a relieved sigh. *Keep close, boys. I think this is where things are going to start to get a little frantic.*

A few minutes later, Lorne pulled up outside St. Paul's Cathedral and sat in the car, waiting for Warrior to ring. He rang within a few seconds, Lorne suspected this was thanks to the information her tail was feeding him.

"Lazy bitch, you couldn't even get out of the car."

"To be fair, you didn't tell me to. What am I looking for this time?"

"Nothing. Now ditch the car and make your way by tube to Madame Tussauds. You have forty minutes, Simpkins."

"There's no way I'll make it there in time."

"Not my problem. Do it, or I'll break a limb on one of the hostages. I'll even let you choose who I hurt first." He laughed and hung up.

Lorne gathered the two phones and locked the car, no doubt leaving it to be towed away. Then she started running for the nearest tube station, the Barbican. Already out of breath, she rang Sean again. "I'm on foot, heading for Madame Tussauds via the tube. Tell Tony." She ended the call without waiting for him to reply and stepped up her pace, thankful not for the first time that day that she'd chosen to wear her trusty trainers.

After swiping her credit card at the turnstile and picking up her ticket, Lorne began her descent into the bowels of London. It was the worst form of transport Warrior could have ordered her to take. Since the 7/7 bombings, she'd made every attempt to avoid using the tube. Her claustrophobia heightened the lower she went, until she finally made it to the station just in time to see the back end of a tube train disappearing into the tunnel. She thumped her fist against her thigh and paced back and forth until the next train arrived.

Lorne stood erect with her back pressed against the wall and observed the many new passengers arriving, amazed by how many people still travelled by tube in spite of the fear of another terrorist attack. *Was it a case of people easily forgetting the loss of life that day, or do people genuinely feel this is the most convenient way to travel around London?* Either way, Lorne's heart rate rose beyond a comfortable level, forcing her to close her eyes and take in a few deep breaths. She opened them again to find a cute little boy of around four tugging at the hem of her jacket. Lorne smiled and crouched to talk to him, "Hello, little man. Can I help you?"

He started to sob. "I've lost my mummy."

Lorne caught the words between his rasping breaths. "Oh, sweetheart, she can't be very far." She took the child's hand, ran back to the stairs, lifted the boy in her arms, and from the fifth step, shouted, "Can I have your attention everyone please? I have a little boy here who has lost his mummy." She stroked the boy's hair back off his crimson face and asked, "What's your name, sweetie?"

"It's... it's Gavin. I want my mummy."

"Gavin, can you remember your surname? Your last name, darling?"

"Gavin Pea... cock."

She addressed the hushed crowd again. "Is there a Mrs. Peacock here?"

To her amazement, no one stepped forward to claim the child. *Shit! What do I do now?* Lorne's gaze landed on Tony's in the crowd. He shrugged and turned his back on her. Conscious of the punishing timeframe she was working under, she bolted up the stairs to the ticket office. "Sorry, you have to help me. This dear little boy has lost his mum. Can you put a call out for a Mrs. Peacock please?"

The beaming black woman stroked the child's face. "Of course I can, sugar."

Lorne glanced over her shoulder expectantly as the woman's voice boomed around them. "I'm sorry. I hate to do this, but I'm late for an appointment already. Would you mind if I left the child here with you?"

Hearing the words, the boy tightened his arms around Lorne's neck. "No. Stay with me. I want my mummy."

The pleading in his eyes yanked on her heartstrings. "I can't, sweetheart. You'll be safe here with the nice lady. Your mummy won't be long, I'm sure."

Lorne tried to untangle herself from his grasp, but the child held firm. *Shit! So much for me coming to the child's rescue, now I'm bloody trapped. What will people think of me if I just dump him here and run? Sod it, I have to, for the Hardys' sake.* Her inner voice seemed to be in as much turmoil as she was.

The boy's face lit up, and he held out his arms to a sobbing petite blonde woman who rushed towards them.

"Oh, Gavin. Where did you go? I'm so sorry. I stopped to buy a ticket at the machine, turned my back on him for a second, and when I looked again, he'd vanished. I've been going out of my mind, searching for the little rascal."

"Maybe you should keep him on a leash," Lorne said, only half-joking. "I found him on the platform."

"My God, really. You, naughty boy. What have I told you about going near the trains by yourself? It's dangerous, Gavin. Very, very dangerous."

"I'm sorry. I've got to fly. I'm late as it is."

"Sorry, of course. Forgive us again. I can't thank you enough for rescuing him."

Lorne touched the woman's arm and kissed the little boy's cheek. "It's all in a day's work. Don't let him out of your sight again. He's far too precious to lose."

Lorne bolted back down the stairs just as another train was pulling into the station. The crowd surged forward, and she felt someone's hand grab hers. Lorne didn't react and continued to move with the crowd to board the train. She knew the warmth of her husband's touch. She squeezed his hand and pushed ahead, through the carriage and placed her back against the carriage wall and held on firmly to the metal railing. Lorne bowed her head, pretending to look at the floor of the carriage, all the time observing those around her, trying to identify the man tailing her, but again, no one stood out in the crowd. Even Tony had disappeared from her sight. Her heart skipped several beats as the train pulled away from the station. *Oh no, what if he and Joe didn't make it?*

She pushed the terrifying thought from her mind and spent the rest of the journey surveying the crowd and promising to give her sister a call. It had been several weeks since they'd last contacted each other. Dealing with the lost child had made her realise how far apart they had grown recently. She would endeavour to put that right once she and the hostages were all back home, safe and sound.

The train drew to a halt, and the passengers disembarked quickly. Lorne caught sight of the back of Tony's head going up the flight of steps ahead of her. Once she was out in the open again, she rushed along Marylebone Road. She stood outside Madame Tussauds, bent over fighting for breath. Her mobile rang. "Hello."

Warrior laughed. "I thought you coppers were supposed to have a medical every year. You sound pretty unfit to me, Simpkins. Good job you ditched that kid. Otherwise, this kid would have been suffering from a broken arm."

"Just tell me what to do now. I've told you I'll comply with your instructions. If I can make the allotted time, I'll do everything in my power to do it."

"Good. I'm glad to hear it. I'm sure the families we have here at the moment—and the one we're about to acquire—will appreciate your efforts come the end."

"What? You're planning to kidnap someone else? Why?"

"You can stop interrogating me, bitch. If you keep up your end of the bargain, then we'll do the same. *We're* in control; not you. Am I making myself perfectly clear?"

"I understand completely. Please, just answer one question for me."

"You can ask it, whether I'll answer it is another matter entirely."

"Why are you jeopardising so many lives? What's your ultimate aim in this?"

"Uh-oh, you got greedy, lady. I said I might answer one question, and you asked two. I guess you're still having trouble figuring out who's in charge here."

Warrior paused, and Lorne heard a door open then a woman scream. "No, please, there's no need for anyone to get harmed."

Another scream filtered down the line, and Lorne chastised herself for goading him unnecessarily. "Recognise who's in charge now, Simpkins?"

"Yes. Okay, what do you want me to look for now?" She tried to distract him from punishing the woman further.

"There's no clue there. We're still going by your suggestions, remember? However, you struck lucky when you named the HOP. You'll find a valuable clue at the Houses of Parliament."

Lorne exhaled loudly.

"Now, you've got exactly thirty minutes to get there."

Lorne turned and sprinted back towards the Baker Street underground station.

Before Warrior hung up, he hit the woman a second time, and she yelled out in pain. "Please help us," the woman screamed.

Lorne swallowed the lump filling her throat and rang Sean at the station. "I'm heading for the HOP, Sean. He's taken to hurting one of the women he's holding if I question him over anything."

"Damn, don't antagonise the shithead, Lorne."

"I'm trying not to. Any news on the vehicles? He's threatened that the hostage count is about to rise."

"Shit, shit, shit! We're following up on two calls regarding the Orion, nothing on the four-by-four yet. Did the kidnapper give you any clue as to who they're going to pounce on next?"

"No. Where is this bloody going to end? We have to find the hideout. Can you call in the police helicopter?"

"I actioned it about thirty minutes ago. They're scouring the outskirts of London, but that's the crux—we don't have a clue in what definitive direction to send them."

Lorne barged past a man and almost sent him tumbling to the ground. "Look where you're going and get off that damn contraption while you're walking," he cursed at her when she pulled him upright.

"Sorry, important business." She headed off again and returned to her conversation. "Sean, the couple of sightings you've received so far—can the chopper not hover around that area? That is, if they're in the vicinity."

"That's the trouble. The two sightings are about thirty miles apart."

"Damn. Are they at least on the same kind of route?"

"How the effing hell should I know? We have no route at the moment."

"Don't take your frustration out on me. Work it out. If you can't do it, then bloody get Katy to do your thinking for you. I've got to go." Lorne cut him off before he could argue. She was furious at the speed the team appeared to be working under her boss's leadership. *If only I could tear myself in two, I could run both sides of the operation then.*

CHAPTER FOURTEEN

Katy could see how furious Sean was when he finished his call with Lorne. She walked up to him and inclined her head. "Is she throwing her weight around again?"

His eyes narrowed. "When isn't she? I'm already regretting giving her your job."

Katy folded her arms and sat on the edge of the desk behind her. "Now I know you're jesting. You'd be lost—*we'd* be lost—without her on the case."

His head hung low, and he shrugged. "I know you're right. She just frustrates the hell out of me at times." He clapped his hands and shook his head as if pulling himself out of his slumber. "Right, where do we stand? The chopper is in the air, right? I think that needs to be our priority."

"It's in the air, but nothing to report yet. It's going to be difficult without having further details of the cars and possible sightings."

Sean nodded. "I agree, and I suspect things are going to get a whole lot trickier, too."

Katy frowned. "How come?"

"Lorne said the kidnapper hinted at yet another family being abducted."

Katy propelled herself off the desk. "What?"

"Yep. Not sure where it's going to end. What I do know is that it's vital we stop these guys."

"What the hell are they playing at? What's their objective?"

"Valid questions that we just haven't found the answers to yet. I know what a severe pain in the arse it is, but we're going to have to start trawling through the CCTV cameras across London."

"Are you crazy? That could take us weeks," Katy protested.

"Then tell me what else we should consider doing, Sergeant. I'm open to all suggestions, no matter how trivial they seem."

Katy sighed. "I hear where you're coming from. Might I suggest that we leave things as they are for the next few hours and concentrate on sifting through the phone calls we've received after the conference aired? The media will be running it again around tea time."

"That's good to hear. Bear in mind that the time limit has shifted, and Hardy has to come up with his ten million by seven this evening," Sean said.

"That's imprinted on my mind, boss." Katy let out a long, suffering breath.

"Let's get cracking then."

***

The muscles in Lorne's legs began to burn as she ran back through the underground in search of the next train on the Jubilee Line that would take her back to the area near where her journey had commenced first thing. She had bought a bottle of water from a street vendor outside the station and downed most of it in one. In the distance, the train was nearing the opening, and Lorne stood back from the platform just in case anyone had any bright ideas about pushing her under the approaching vehicle. *Don't be daft! They need me. I've been watching too many high-octane thrillers on TV lately.*

Again, she did her obligatory discreet scout around the surrounding area and thought she saw a man she recognised from a few other destinations, but then, knowing how her luck had tested her that day, she feared her assumption was totally off the mark. She did manage to catch a glimpse of Joe at the back of the crowd. He winked at her and motioned with his head that Tony was within spitting distance. Lorne presumed her hubby was taking a toilet break. She feared she'd need to do the same thing before long if she downed any more full bottles of water the way she had.

The train came to a halt in front of the crowd, and the doors *whooshed* open. The people moved swiftly, like a large swarm of bees heading back to the hive after a successful pollen-hunting trip. Lorne hopped in the first carriage and sought out her usual spot, cautious of facing the crowd instead of turning her back on them. As the train pulled out of the station and into the tunnel, Lorne glanced sideways at the blackness outside. She caught a glimpse in the window of a man scrutinising her. Pretending she hadn't seen him, she looked away but continued to watch him in her peripheral vision. He seemed contemplative, as if he were going over a plan in his head. Lorne's stomach muscles matched her legs—both constricted nervously. The fifteen-minute journey felt unending. She leapt out of the train at Westminster Underground Station and ran ahead of the surging pack. Out in the open, she sprinted until the huge building she was in search of lay ahead of her. She waited at the perimeter of the Houses of Parliament for more instructions from the kidnapper.

Her phone rang. "Yes."

"Go to the entrance at the front of the building. Look for the nearest bench. Underneath that bench, you'll find what you're after." Warrior abruptly ended the call.

Lorne ran as fast as her legs would carry her. She stood at the entrance and cast her eyes around. Her heart sank when she spotted more than four benches in the immediate vicinity. She approached the first one cautiously and got down on her knees to look beneath the bench, she pretended to be tying her shoe laces, only to be disappointed. Rising to her feet again, she sought out the next bench and did the same. This time, she found a brown package. *Shit! What if it's a bloody bomb, and it's been rigged to go off if I touch it?* Her nerves shattered when her phone rang and Warrior's taunting laughter greeted her.

"What's the matter, Simpkins? Think it's going to go *bang?*"

"No. Not at all."

"That's not what 'my eyes on the ground' are telling me. Pick it up. It would be a waste to dispose of you in such a crude way."

Lorne hesitated for a split second, swallowed the bile that had crept into her throat, then tore into the package while still crouched on the ground, her phone pinned between her shoulder and her ear. Inside the parcel, she found a mobile phone. She closed her eyes and chewed the inside of her cheek. *I know what he's going to say next.*

"Done it? What do you see?"

"A mobile. What do you want me to do with it?"

"Use it. Dump your other two and stop fucking treating me like an idiot."

"I'm not. I swear."

"You can effing swear all you like. I know you're being tailed by that ex-spy husband of yours. I also assume that your boss left you his mobile to keep in contact with the station. Am I right?"

Lorne stood up and sighed. "Yes, you're right."

"Like I said, don't treat me like a fucking moron, Simpkins. Doesn't it bother you that your actions carry severe consequences for the families I'm holding?"

"Of course. I'm sorry. I can't say any more than that. This is my mistake, not the people you are holding captive. Any punishment you plan on dishing out should be directed at me, not them."

"You're un-fucking-believable! Still dishing out orders in spite of the situation. I'm going to say this once and once only, Simpkins."

"I'm listening. I promise I'll play the game by your rules from now on."

"Good. Glad we're clear on that, *finally*. Now dump your frigging phones and get back on the tube."

Lorne's shoulders slumped. "What? Where to now?"

"Head over to the Museum of London. This will be your final stop."

"Okay, I'm on my way."

"Yeah, alone this time and at breakneck speed. You need to do all you can to dodge your hubby, got that?"

"How long have I got?"

"Thirty-five minutes, tops! If you screw this up, one of the hostages will definitely be killed."

He hung up. Lorne dumped her own mobile and Sean's under the bench and tucked the new phone she'd acquired in her pocket then bolted for the underground again. She could see out of the corner of her eye the man Warrior had strapped to her as a tail, but didn't have a clue where either Tony or Joe were. *Shit! This time, I'm well and truly screwed.* As she ran, she sent out a prayer for her guardian angel not to desert her. *Pete, if you're around, I need you to watch my back big time, chunky. I miss you, buddy.*

Something fluttered to the ground in front of her, and she stopped to pick it up. She tucked the white feather in her pocket and looked up at the building beside her to see a pigeon sitting on a ledge, preening itself. Seeing it as some sort of sign, she whispered, "That'll do for me."

She wiped away the tears filling her eyes and bolted at full pelt until she reached the station she'd arrived at around fifteen minutes earlier. With the feeling of déjà vu at the forefront of her mind, she swiped her credit card, grabbed a ticket and descended into the depths of the underground once again, aware of the man she'd picked out as her likely follower right behind her. She prayed that Tony and Joe were somewhere near them, too.

***

"What do you mean she's on her own, Tony?"

"Just that, mate. She picked up a parcel, opened it and withdrew a mobile. He knew we were following her, and is now calling the shots, not that he wasn't doing that already. Don't worry, I picked up the phones she dumped."

Sean could hear how breathless Tony was. "And? Have you still got her in your sight?"

"That's a negative, Sean. She took off as if she had a torpedo strapped to her arse. I sent Joe on ahead of me because of my leg restrictions. I have no idea if he's managed to keep up with her or not."

"Bloody hell, Tony! What are we supposed to do now?"

"Don't have a go at me, mate. We need to think positive about this. Lorne's not stupid. Her main priority will be to those families, not protecting her own life. Maybe the kidnapper threatened to kill one of the hostages, and that's why she did everything she could to ditch us."

"Perhaps you're right. What are you going to do now?"

"Stay out here, I suppose. I'll head towards the tube station, see if Joe is around. I'm hoping I won't find him."

"Okay. I'm going to issue orders for uniforms on the street to keep an eye out for her."

"Be careful about doing that. These blokes might be listening in on the police channel. I wouldn't put it past them."

"You're right." Sean kicked out at a chair. "What a fuck-up! What's worse is that this Warrior intimated that another family is about to be snatched."

"Shit!"

"Yeah, shit! We haven't heard anything regarding any possible new abductions. There's every chance he could have just been saying it to keep us on our toes."

"That's unlikely, going by the threats he's fulfilled in the past. Look, I'll keep checking in when and if I hear anything at this end, if you'll do the same."

"That goes without saying." Sean hung up and turned to Katy. "Looks like Lorne's out there on her own."

Katy shook her head in disbelief. "Not for long. We need to put our heads together and get serious about this, Sean. I refuse to have Lorne's disappearance or death on my conscience."

He was taken aback by Katy's abrupt manner. "That's rather harsh, Sergeant."

"It's what Lorne would say if the tables were turned."

AJ was on the phone, waving at them to gain their attention. Katy and Sean joined him. AJ ended his call and handed Sean the piece of paper. "That's the confirmation we needed. They've struck again."

Sean ground his teeth. "Right, if they can do it, then so can we. Katy, I want you and AJ to visit the crime scene. Take a few uniformed officers with you. Let's get over there ASAP before any witnesses disappear into the bloody ether."

AJ pushed back his chair, slipped on his jacket, then followed Katy out of the incident room.

"I'm on it," she called back over her shoulder.

"Ask anyone and everyone, AJ, even the dogs in that area if you have to. Let's do all that we can to track these bastards down. I'll contact the husband from this end."

"What? Over the phone?" AJ asked, sounding as though he disapproved of Sean's suggestion.

"Yes. We haven't got the manpower to keep sending people out to see folks. We need to concentrate our efforts on finding this gang and the hostages they have already before they grab half the residents in London."

AJ nodded and sprinted after Katy.

CHAPTER FIFTEEN

Katy and AJ arrived at the golf club to find a throng of people waiting for them. Some were dressed in golfing attire and leaning on their golf bags, and others appeared to be members of the club staff.

A man wearing a black suit and an anxious expression approached them. "Are you the police?"

"We are indeed. DS Katy Foster and DS Alan Jackson. Are you Mr. Wallace?"

"Yes, I'm the manager here. I placed the call as soon as the woman and her child were taken."

"Did anyone else see the incident?" Katy asked, scanning the crowd.

"Yes, a few of us. We tried to intervene, but the men threatened us with guns."

Katy and AJ exchanged worried glances. "Was anyone hurt?" Katy asked.

"No, only our prides for being so useless."

"Don't feel bad. Can you give us a description of the men? Or how many there were?"

"There were three men, and no, I can't tell you what they looked like as they wore balaclavas."

"Hmm… that's not really helpful. Perhaps you heard one of them call one of his associates by name?"

"No, not that I can remember."

Katy asked the crowd, "Did anyone hear one of them mention a name?"

The crowd shook their heads. Katy feared as much. Nothing seemed to be going their way. "What about the vehicle? Did anyone get the number plate?"

Mr. Wallace thought for a moment then shook his head. "Do you know what? I don't think the vehicle had one."

"Really? That's not what I was expecting to hear."

"What vehicle was it?" Katy asked.

"A black four-by-four. I didn't catch the make, sorry."

"Can you tell us a little about the woman who was taken?"

"She's the wife of one of our directors, Sarah Lockhart. She'd just called in to see how the arrangements were going for her husband's fiftieth birthday party."

"I see, and when is the party due to take place?"

"This weekend. Her child was screaming." The man shuddered. "The pair of them were terrified, reaching out for us to help them. We couldn't do a damn thing. A few of us attempted to grab the child, but Tommy over there got a thrashing from one of the blokes."

Katy glanced at the young man, who had blood running down his face. "He should go to the hospital, get that seen to."

"He'll go eventually. He wanted to hang around until you guys came. We're all eager to give you as much information as we can to help you arrest these men and to get the family found as soon as possible. Why would anyone kidnap them like this?"

"That's what we're trying to work out, Mr. Wallace. How long ago did the incident happen? An exact time would help."

The man tutted. "I suppose about thirty to forty minutes ago. Everything is such a blur."

Katy addressed the crowd. "Anyone know an exact time?"

"Like Ray just said, about thirty to forty minutes, I think," a man in red tartan trousers replied.

AJ took notes while Katy continued asking the questions. "Did anyone see the direction the car took off in?"

Mr. Wallace pointed at the main road. "They turned right, if that helps."

"It does. Thanks. Did the men hurt either Mrs. Lockhart or her daughter?"

"Not that I could tell. Yes, they manhandled them into the back of the vehicle, but that was about it as far as we could see. That's right, folks, isn't it?"

The crowd nodded their agreement in unison.

Katy turned to AJ and said, "There's not a lot else we can do here." Addressing Mr. Wallace again, she added, "We'll leave the two uniformed officers here. They'll take down all your statements, and we'll continue our investigation back at the station."

"Sorry we couldn't help more."

"If you think of anything else, please, ring me." Katy fished a business card out of her pocket and offered it to the man.

He took the card and popped it in his trouser pocket. "Thanks. There really isn't anything else. Please, do your best to rescue Mrs. Lockhart and her child. I hate to think that kind of thing occurred here. We've never dealt with anything like this before, and in broad daylight, too."

"We'll do our best. Thanks for your help, all of you," Katy said, giving the crowd a brief smile.

She and AJ returned to the car.

"Looks like this gang are keen to show they mean business," AJ said, turning the key in the ignition.

"I think they've showed us that right from day one, AJ. Let's hope the chopper locates that address soon. I fear it's going to be our only way of stopping them."

"I think you're right. Back to the station?"

"Take the same route out of here as the kidnappers. Let's see what we find down this road."

The answer turned out to be a big fat zero, so they continued back to the station.

***

Warrior watched the men unload the woman and child. "Take them down to the cellar. The rats are lonely," he ordered. The woman's eyes extended in fear, and he laughed. "I don't think they've eaten for a while."

The child tried to reach for her mother and cried out, "Mummy, please don't let them hurt me."

Her mother glared at him, and he challenged her with his head cocked to the side. "Are you going to save your little princess, Mummy?"

She held his gaze for a second or two longer then smiled at her daughter. "Do as they say, Tara baby, and these nice men won't hurt us."

"Wise words for a rich bitch. Let's hope hubby comes up with the money quickly to get you out of this mess, eh?"

"He will. He loves us."

Warrior chuckled. "How many times have we heard that over the years, boys? Only for the husbands to turn round and say, 'Do what you want to them. I don't give a shit' Eh?"

The three men laughed and pushed the girl and her mother into the house and down the creaking staircase, through the wilderness of thick cobwebs to the seating area they had laid out for the visitors. Two chairs sat side by side with ropes lying on each of the seats.

"Sit," Warrior ordered.

The woman tried again to reassure her child that they wouldn't be hurt if she did as she was told. "Be brave, sweetie." Their hands were tied behind their backs around the chairs, the woman's tighter than the child's.

"Yeah, be brave, girlie. You're going to need to be," Warrior said, pointing at something that moved in the corner of the room.

The girl screamed when the rat's eyes glowed in the darkness.

"Let's get out of here and leave our visitors to make acquaintances with the other inmates." Warrior laughed, and the four men left the room, closing the door behind them, ensuring their visitors were thrust into complete darkness. The woman and child screamed again.

Warrior sighed and headed back into the kitchen, where the infant child was yelling once more. "Jesus, this place is getting more and more like a crèche with every passing hour. Go and get the woman to see to her child, Spike."

Spike left the house, returned with a terrified and filthy Bethany a few moments later, and untied her hands so she could feed her baby. "Deal with the sprog. Not long now, bitch."

"Has my husband paid the ransom money?"

"Not yet. He's got about six hours to come up with the dosh, or you and the kid get buried together, *alive*."

Bethany gasped and grabbed her child, cradling him in her arms. "You don't mean that."

"Don't I? We'll see, eh? The countdown to your demise has begun in earnest, lady. It all depends on how much your husband values your lives if you get out of this scenario alive."

"Please, let me try and persuade him to get the money together. We're not as wealthy as you think we are."

"Who the fuck are you trying to kid, lady? I saw your mansion, remember?"

"You saw a home that has a one hundred percent mortgage on it. My husband works over eighty hours a week to try and recover the money we lost in a big contract."

"Yeah, we've all got sob stories like that we can bandy about. Take me, for instance—I've just booked a two-week holiday in the Bahamas, but I ain't got two beans to rub together to pay for it. I will have, when your hubby stomps up the ten mill, though." His head fell backwards as he cackled.

"How can you do this? Treat people no better than if they were animals?"

He took a few steps towards her and touched her nose with his. "Stop questioning me and my motives, lady. Some of us have to work hard in this life to achieve what we have today."

"That's us. We work hard. Seven days a week. My husband hasn't had a holiday in five years because he's always striving to make the business flourish and grow. The money, when it comes our way, doesn't just fall from the trees in our back garden, you know."

"I've warned you once to shut your mouth—now *do* it." His fist connected with her jaw, and she stumbled back against the wall but didn't loosen her grip on the baby.

Hatred filled her eyes, then suddenly she turned away from him and ran for the door. The men in the room stood and watched her hand tremble as she fumbled with the doorknob. She managed to get the door open, only for her attempt to be thwarted as another one of Warrior's men blocked her path. She beat his chest with her free arm. He swivelled her in place and shoved her back into the house. "That's it. I'm done with you, bitch. Take your effing kid with you and get back in that bloody pit where you belong."

Warrior clutched a handful of her hair and dragged her through the back door. She was yelling and clawing at his arm while her child's crying escalated to an even higher level than it had reached previously. He opened the door, latched onto her free arm, twisted it, and lowered her into the hole. "You're going to stay there indefinitely now. No food or water, *nothing*. I'll teach you to respect me, woman. You hear me?"

"Yes," she muttered quietly as she descended into the wooden hole.

Warrior slammed the doors shut and applied the bolt. In the distance, he thought he heard something but had trouble distinguishing what the noise was. Angry, he stormed back into the house and picked up the phone.

***

Lorne snatched the ringing phone from her pocket and answered the call.

"Simpkins, where are you?"

Lorne paused her running to speak to the kidnapper. "I'm almost there now. What do I look for?"

"I'll give you another two minutes to get there."

Lorne looked at the phone then quickly tucked it in her jacket pocket as if to avoid it burning through the palm of her hand. The crowd was thick in front of her, so Lorne left the pavement and ran in the kerb of the road. Traffic had virtually ground to a standstill anyway, so she didn't have to contend with the extra worry of a speeding car knocking her over.

Moments later, she reached the steps of the incredible building that housed all of London's past under one roof. She waited outside the front door for Warrior to ring. Her foot started to tap, and she anxiously checked her phone.

Finally, he rang.

"Hello."

"Are you there?"

"I'm here."

"Right, I want you to make your way inside the building and head for the Crime Museum. Lucky this was one of the places you picked out earlier, because I've 'planted' something inside for you to find."

A cold, sinister laugh rippled down the line. "Sounds ominous. Care to give me an extra clue?"

"Nope. Just get in there and go towards the Jack the Ripper exhibit. You have ten minutes."

He hung up, and Lorne joined the small queue at the door, waiting to gain access to the museum. When it was her turn to step through the doorway, she shuddered at the sense of history the building held. *Stay focused! I haven't got time to linger.* She rushed past all the ancient Roman artefacts close to the entrance and tried to locate the signage that would lead her to the appropriate area she needed to conclude her quest. Perplexed, she studied the signs but found no mention of the Crime Museum. Lorne walked over to the reception area.

The woman sitting behind the desk greeted her warmly, "Hello there, how can I help you?"

"I've been told to, er… meet someone at the Crime Museum. Only I can't find any mention of it on the signs."

"That's because it's still being created. The exhibition is due to be opened to the public in October 2015. You're a few months early, I'm afraid."

Panic forced Lorne's mouth to drop open.

"Are you all right? You look as though you've just seen a ghost."

"Yes, I mean, no. I'm sorry. Is it possible to point me in the direction anyway? I'll take a look around for my friend there."

"Of course. Here, take one of these. It'll give you a better idea of where you're going." The receptionist handed Lorne a glossy brochure opened up to a map of the museum. On it, she had circled the area designated for the Crime Museum.

"That's brilliant. Thank you so much for your help."

"It's a pleasure. I hope you find your friend."

Lorne smiled and walked swiftly through the corridors of history, promising herself that she would bring Charlie and Tony for a visit one day in the near future—if she got out of the situation alive.

After arriving at the sectioned-off area, she paced the hallway, until finally, Warrior called back.

"You lied," she said, instantly regretting her outburst.

"I told you I would keep you on your toes, Simpkins." He laughed, imitating a dastardly villain from a 1930s horror film.

"I'm glad you think torturing people and messing with their heads is a fun exercise for you. I have to inform you that I'm finding it all a tad boring."

"Oh you are, are you? Okay, I'm sure you'll find your next trip far more exciting. Oh, and by the way, you know I mentioned this would be your last stop? That *huge* mouth of yours just extended your little adventure."

Lorne's shoulders slumped, and tears of frustration pricked her eyes. *Keep your trap shut, girl!*

Refusing to let on how disappointed she felt, she stretched, pulled her shoulders back, and said, "Bring it on, buster. Bring it on."

Warrior growled, forcing a smile to break out across her face. "Get on a river cruise," he said.

"What? You need to give me more than that."

"Go to the Thames Circular Cruise. You've got thirty minutes."

"Wait!" she cried, but it was too late. *Crap! I have no idea where that sets off from.*

She retraced her steps back through the corridors to the receptionist.

"Any luck?" the woman asked, smiling.

"No. I rang her, and she's been held up. She suggested that we meet at the Thames Circular Cruise. I have no idea where that is. My friend's phone died before she could give me directions. Can you help at all?"

The woman left her seat and walked over to a large display rack housing an abundance of tourist leaflets. She picked one off the top row before returning to Lorne and placing it on the counter in front of her. "There you are. All the information you require should be in there."

"You've saved my life for a second time today. I'm extremely grateful. Thank you."

"No problem. Enjoy the rest of your day."

If only you knew what I'm up against!

CHAPTER SIXTEEN

Katy and AJ returned to the station after their disappointing trip to the crime scene. Sean greeted them with a raised eyebrow and a twinkle in his eye.

"Sir? I take it you have some good news."

"I think so. It's yet to be confirmed, but I think we might have located the gang's hideout."

"Are you sure? That's excellent news. Where?" Katy's heart pounded against her ribs.

"The chopper is circulating the area now, discreetly of course. Looks like a disused farm. One of the crew thinks he spotted a four-by-four poking out of one of the barns. Seems strange having such a smart vehicle at a farm no longer in use, doesn't it?"

"I agree." Katy followed Sean over to the whiteboard. He pointed at an area on the map close to Epping in Essex. "That seems pretty remote, although definitely feasible. What's the next step?"

"I've asked the chopper to come back and pick me up. I want to get out there and see for myself what we're up against before we contemplate sending reinforcements out there. I'd hate to look foolish if it turned out to be a mistake."

"Makes sense. Do you need anyone to go with you?"

"No. You stay here and man the phones in case Lorne or Tony make contact. I'll assess the situation thoroughly then call for back-up."

"Okay. Can I tell you to be cautious, though? The last thing we want to do is alert them. Don't forget there are hostages at stake here."

"Thanks for that reminder, Sergeant. I have all the necessary teams on alert. Once I get the clarification I need, I'll contact those teams direct, and we'll hit the location en masse. Is that how you would play it if you were still in charge?"

Katy's cheeks heated up under his glare. "Yes, boss. That's exactly the route I would have taken if I were in your position. What news of Lorne? Anything?"

"Nope. Nothing at all. I haven't heard from Tony since his last call, either. I'm hoping he's in contact with Joe and that Joe has eyes on Lorne."

"It's certainly a logistical nightmare. I have a feeling that was this Warrior's intention from the word *go*. What about the husband of the latest kidnapped family? What's he had to say about things?"

"He's distraught, of course, and is trying to secure the funds he needs for the expected ransom demand, which by the way, still hasn't been made."

"I take it you told him it would be ten million?"

"Going by the other two demands, that's the assumption I made. Knowing this Warrior's mind, though, I wouldn't put it past him to alter things. Look at the futile game he's been playing with Lorne all day."

"I hear you. When's the chopper due back?" Katy asked.

"Anytime now. I'm going to head up to the roof and wait for it to land. Keep on top of everything here until I return, okay?"

"Yes, boss." Katy watched Sean dash out of the room, envious that she hadn't been asked to go along for the ride. *Have I done the right thing, accepting a demotion? My head says yes. However, my heart says no.*

She felt a hand rub her arm and smiled when she found AJ looking down at her. "I know what you're feeling, the doubts you're having. It's for the best, Katy. Your talents are required at this end. This part of the investigation will benefit immensely from your leadership skills."

"You've done it again."

He frowned slightly. "What?"

"You've made me feel wanted, appreciated, when I was beginning to doubt myself."

"That's what partners are for, and there's no need for you to ever doubt yourself. You'll adjust to your predicament soon enough. Lorne won't treat you any differently. You know that."

Katy sighed and looked him in the eye. "What if she doesn't return, AJ? What if this time she really has put her life in jeopardy?"

AJ threw an arm around her shoulder and hugged her to his chest. "She'll be fine. Your fears will turn out to be unfounded; I know they will. Have faith in her abilities. She's been in worse scrapes than this over the years."

"I know. Just blame my hormones for me wearing my sentimental head. Right, back to it."

"What do you want me to do?"

"Carry on with what you were doing before we left, I suppose." Katy followed AJ back to his chair then made a detour to speak to Karen. "I'm assuming that DCI Roberts asked you to look into this farm?"

"He did, boss. I'm doing the background checks on it now. The records show that the farm was last owned by a Donald Fryatt, who sadly died at the beginning of 2014."

"I see. Any living relatives?"

"As far as I can tell, just the one—Jamie Fryatt, who lives in Waltham Abbey."

"Good. Have you rung him?"

"No, boss. I've only just uncovered the information. Would you like me to do that now?"

"I'll do it. Do you have the details?"

Karen slipped a piece of paper into Katy's outstretched hand. Katy stepped over to the vending machine, thought about buying a cup of coffee, then veered off at the last moment and headed towards the water container on the other side of the room. Water in hand, she settled behind Lorne's desk in the office and dialled the number.

"Hello," an abrupt voice answered.

"Is that Mr. Jamie Fryatt?"

"It is. If you're selling double glazing, we had it installed last year. And I'm not interested in solar panels, so do one!"

Katy chortled. "I'm not. I'm DS Katy Foster from the Met police. I'm ringing up to see if you can give me any information on the farm that used to belong to Mr. Donald Fryatt. Was that your father?"

"No, it was my uncle's place. What about it? Do you want to buy it? It's for sale at a knocked-down price. I'm still willing to take an offer on it."

"Sorry to mislead you. No, I'm not interested in buying it. Have you visited the place lately?"

"No. Why? Damn, has it been vandalised? Is that what you're working up to, Sergeant?"

"Not as far as I know. I repeat, have you been there lately?"

"I haven't. I don't see how that would be of concern to the police, though."

"Just bear with me, if you will. Does anyone else in your family have access to the farm?"

"Not at all. I'm the sole beneficiary," he replied quickly. "Lady, you're getting me worried now. What's going on?"

Cagily, Katy said, "That's the problem—we're not sure if anything is going on up there or not. I'm just making general enquiries about empty properties on our patch."

"Ah, I see. Well, that makes sense, what with the level of today's crime statistics."

"Exactly. Thanks for your help, Mr. Fryatt. No doubt we'll be in contact again in a few months. Hopefully, you'll have sold it by then."

"Here's hoping."

Katy hung up then rang Sean on AJ's mobile that he'd borrowed. Katy heard the noise of the helicopter and shouted, "Boss, I've contacted the owner of the farm."

"And what did he say, Sergeant?"

"I pretended we were checking up on vacant properties in the area, and as far as he's concerned, no one should be out there."

"Okay, thanks for the heads-up. Standby; I'll contact you when I get there."

"Roger that," Katy said.

***

Tony was searching the immediate area around the tube station, mainly checking to make sure Joe hadn't received a bump on the head from one of Warrior's goons, when his mobile rang. Without looking at the number, he answered it. "Thank Christ, I was worried. Where are you?"

"I'm at the house, Tony."

"Sorry, who is this? Carol, is that you?"

"Yes. Something has happened."

"Such as?" His head swivelled as he surveyed the area.

"She's gone... they came and took her... I couldn't stop them."

Tony ran his free hand through his greying hair, and fear tightened his chest. "What are you trying to tell me, Carol?"

"Charlie. Two men turned up... oh, I don't know, about thirty minutes ago and took her." Carol began to sob.

"Calm down, love. You need to give me all the facts."

"We were out in the kennels, seeing to the dogs, and fancied a cuppa. When we came in the back door, two men were sitting at the kitchen table. We tried our hardest to fight them off, Tony. Even Sheba got kicked out of the way when she tried to prevent them from taking Charlie."

"Shit! Carol. She was supposed to be safe with you. Sorry, that wasn't meant to come out like that."

"It's okay. I tried to protect her, but they knocked me out, Tony. I've just come round, and you're the first person I thought about ringing."

"I'm glad, love. Are you all right? Do you want me to come back to the house?"

"No! Don't you dare! I'm fine. I'll take care of Sheba and me. You stay out there. How's Lorne doing?"

Tony tutted. "I've lost her, Carol. We got separated, and the kidnapper made her dump all communications she had with us."

"Oh no! So, these men have both Lorne and Charlie now? What will happen? Is Katy aware of this? Sorry, of course she is."

"Yes, everyone is aware. Don't worry. I'm hoping that Joe is still on her tail; we also got separated."

"Have you tried to contact him? He has got a mobile, hasn't he?"

"Yes, I've tried. His phone is either switched off or on silent. I'm sure he'll realise soon and get in touch. I'm hoping that'll be the case anyway."

"I hope so, too. I better get off the phone in case he's trying to get in touch. Will you call me if you hear anything?"

"Of course. You sit there and take it easy. I'm sorry you were hurt, Carol. Let me get in touch with Katy now, all right?"

"You do that. Take care. Bring my girls back home to me, alive."

"That's the plan, love." Tony ended the call and immediately dialled Katy's mobile. "Hi, Katy. It's me again. Carol's just rung me. Charlie has been kidnapped."

He heard a chair scraping across the floor.

"Holy shit! How?"

"She was at the kennels with Carol. Two men attacked them, knocked Carol out, and took off with Charlie."

"When was this?"

"Carol thinks it was around thirty minutes ago."

"That's around the same time we lost all contact with Lorne."

Tony slammed a fist into his thigh. "Yes, Christ! What do we do now, Katy?"

"Hang tight, mate. Sean's just taken off to check a possible hideout where we think the kidnappers might be holding the hostages."

"That's brilliant news. Where?"

"It's a fair way out in Epping. We have the response teams on standby. We're just waiting for Sean to give us the go-ahead before we instigate any form of attack. Do we know what car they used to pick up Charlie?"

"No, Carol didn't say."

"That's going to make it difficult to pinpoint the vehicle, then. Although, my guess is that these men will probably end up back at the farm with Charlie."

"I'm inclined to think the same. Shit, I feel so damn useless. On the one hand, I think I should remain out here in case Joe rings, and on the other, I think I should be there with you guys when things kick off."

"You'd be welcome here, Tony. You know that, but maybe it would be better if you remained out in the field for now, eh?"

"Agreed. I'll keep ringing Joe. He's gotta pick up some time, hasn't he?"

"I would have thought so. It's a shame you didn't think about putting some form of tracking device on either Lorne or Joe."

"The thought crossed my mind, too. Don't worry. We never anticipated the kidnapper telling her to dump her phone. We should have factored that into the equation, and I'll be kicking myself for not anticipating that forever more."

"We don't have time for recriminations and self-admonishment. Let's do what we can to bring Lorne and Charlie back home, unharmed."

"I'll shoot off and try to contact Joe again."

"You do that. Keep in touch."

Tony hung up and dialled Joe's mobile. It rang once and then went into voicemail. *What's wrong with his damn phone? Is it because he's on the underground?* He left an urgent message for Joe to return his call, then put his phone in his pocket. He rubbed his aching leg, fearing that his stump would show signs of blistering before the day was out. But that was the least of his worries. His wife and child were missing, and he didn't have the slightest idea how to find them. Maybe it was time to call in reinforcements. The next call he made was one that he thought he would never be forced to make again.

CHAPTER SEVENTEEN

The chopper swept low across the fields, then, when the location drew closer, climbed higher in the sky. Sean's gaze was trained on the open fields ahead, which were dotted with the odd farmhouse or barn. The pilot spoke to him through his headphones, "Not long now, sir."

Sean replied with a thumbs-up. A few seconds later, the pilot nudged him in the ribs and pointed to the left as the chopper took a wide sweep around the farm's perimeter. He offered Sean a pair of binoculars.

Sean peered through the lenses, and his gaze immediately caught the tail end of the Orion poking out of a barn close to the old, ramshackled farmhouse. He asked the pilot to circle a second time. Out of the corner of his eye, he saw a cloud of dust approaching the property. Sean urged the pilot to take the chopper higher to avoid being seen, but it was too late. The four-by-four drew up in the drive. Two men got out, and another man came out of the back door of the property to greet them.

The three men covered their eyes from the glare of the sun and focused on the chopper.

"Uh-oh, looks like we've been made. Can you speed up and get us out of here?" Sean ordered the pilot just as the men below took out their weapons and opened fire on the chopper. Sean fished AJ's mobile out of his pocket and dialled the station. "Katy, we're under attack. I haven't got time to make another call. Ring the Armed Response Team I have on standby. Tell them to storm the place now!" Metal pinged as a bullet hit the side of the chopper. "Jesus, we've got to get out of here. Shit!"

"Sean... Sean, what is it?"

"Crap, Katy, unless my eyes are deceiving me, a vehicle has just pulled up, and the men are dragging *Charlie* from the car."

"Shit! Well, at least we know where she is."

"What? You *knew*?"

"Yes, only just. Tony rang a few minutes ago. Are you sure you want to send an ART in there, Sean?"

"What else do you suggest? Negotiators? I don't think these guys are much into having a conversation with us. Just make the call and let the commanding officer decide. Make him aware of what hostages we believe are present, okay?"

"Doing it now. Are you on your way back?"
"Yes... we'll tr..."

***

"Sean? Sean, can you hear me?" The line was dead. Katy dialled the number of the ART unit and actioned Sean's request for back-up. Then she called Tony. "Tony, it's Katy. Listen, Sean's rung. The men spotted him at the location, and they've fired shots at him."

"Bloody hell. Is he okay?"

"I have no idea—the line went dead. I have a response team on the way. Look, there's something you should know."

"What is it, Katy?"

She let out a huge sigh. "Before I lost contact with Sean, he told me he saw Charlie getting out of a vehicle."

"Fuck! So they have got her. I wonder what they have lined up for Lorne. I'm hoping they lead her there, too, to be with Charlie."

"I doubt that will happen. Look, I have to go. The super will be furious if I don't tell her Sean has gone MIA."

"You do that. Keep me posted, Katy."

"I will."

***

Tony rotated on the spot, torn by what direction to take. His mobile rang, postponing his decision. "Hello?"

"Jesus, man! I've been ringing you for ages."

"Shit, Joe, likewise. Your bloody phone kept going into voicemail. Where are you?"

"Down by the river. Looks like Lorne's being forced to take a boat ride."

Tony ran as fast as his aching limbs would carry him along the bustling pavement to the underground station at the top of the road.

"Whereabouts?"

"We're at Tower Pier."

"I'm on my way. Try and keep in contact with me, mate."

"Just get here."

"Going into the tube station now. Joe, the gang have abducted Charlie, Lorne's daughter. Lorne's boss is at the location where they suspect the hostages are being held. The kidnappers have weapons. My guess is that they'll try and make a run for it."

"Jesus, sorry, man! Do you think they'll take the hostages with them?"

"Yep, it would be pointless to leave them behind. I'm glad Lorne is out of contact and unaware of Charlie's plight, but I fear the kidnapper will probably goad her with the information soon enough. That's going to bloody destroy her."

"What mother wouldn't be affected by such news? Tony, she's got through this once before. They both have. We'll get them out of this, mate. Don't worry."

"Let's effing well hope so. I'll be with you shortly." Tony disconnected the call and sprinted through the station and onto the platform. His mind raced at a hundred miles an hour until the train pulled to a stop in front of him.

***

Lorne arrived at the Westminster pier and stood in line with dozens of tourists, who seemed to be speaking every language known to man. With the drone of their voices in the background, she continued to survey the area, aware that Warrior probably had his eagle-eyed sidekick scrutinising her every move. For the last couple of hours, she had felt alone and out in the wilderness, wishing that Tony had kept up with her. Then she'd spotted Joe, disguised under a peaked cap, at the end of the queue. Her heart skipped several beats when she realised that she was no longer alone. *But where is Tony? Oh God, has something gone wrong? Has he been involved in an accident?* She shuddered and looked over to her left to find a man observing her through narrowed eyes. *That's him. It has to be.* His gaze swiftly averted, and she followed suit, not wishing to let on that she'd identified him.

The crew welcomed the passengers aboard the cruiser, and Lorne moved with the surging crowd, still keeping an eye on her surroundings. Something drew her attention to the car park, making her pulse race as if it belonged to an Olympic marathon runner. *Thank God!* Tony sought out Joe, high-fived his partner, and looked directly at her. Her cheeks warmed under his familiar loving gaze. Feeling secure once more, she boarded the boat with the rest of the passengers and chose one of the seats close to the side of the boat. Tony and Joe sat a few seats ahead of her, and the man following her sat close to the cabin of the cruiser. *Why? Is he intending to take over the boat at some point during the journey?* Maybe that was her overactive imagination at play. However, she vowed to be aware of the possibility during the trip.

The crew unhitched the boat from its mooring, and the craft began its cruise down the river. Lorne couldn't help but chuckle when she heard the number of gasps the small group of Japanese tourists exuded as the tour guide pointed out each of the historical landmarks.

In spite of the leisurely journey, she found it impossible to relax, and her stomach remained tied in knots as she contemplated what Warrior had in store for her as his endgame. *There has to be one, doesn't there?* She found it perplexing that he hadn't contacted her again before she'd boarded the boat. Lorne exhaled a breath, unsure whether her questions would be answered anytime soon.

CHAPTER EIGHTEEN

Warrior ordered his men to keep firing at the helicopter, forcing it to vacate the farm, while he rang the boss of the operation.

"We're in the shit."

His boss tutted. "What? Tell me what's happened? Is that gunfire?"

"Yes, boss. We think the hideaway has been discovered."

"By the police? Spit it out, man. Tell me what's going on there. I hope the hostages haven't been harmed."

"No. The hostages are mostly in the house, unharmed. There's only one outside. I'll drag her in here in a sec. We need to get out of here before the police descend on us in force."

"How did they find the location? Did the men screw up? Were they followed?"

"I don't know. You said this copper had her wits about her. Maybe we've underestimated her abilities to our cost."

"Stop being such a defeatist." He mumbled something in his native tongue. "Okay, you've got the truck there, yes?"

"Yes. We haven't used it yet. So as far as I know, they're unaware we have one."

"Well, they'll know if the chopper sees it. Shoot it out of the sky and then make your move. Throw the hostages in the truck and get out of there ASAP. Let me think about this for a few minutes. I'll get back to you soon with a new plan. What about Simpkins?"

"She's on-board a cruiser on the Thames. They've just set off. She'll be tied up for the next forty-five minutes or thereabouts."

"Good. That gives us enough time to alter things around and make new arrangements. Your priority has to be to get out of there within five to ten minutes, but first, you need to shoot that chopper down. Got that?"

"We'll do our best. Although, it looks like it'll soon be out of reach."

"What, from your *guns?* Use your head, man. You've got hundreds of weapons in your possession—*use* them! I'll contact you soon."

Warrior went outside to see how his men were progressing. He covered his eyes against the sun's glare and saw the chopper just dipping out of sight behind a nearby hill. He raked a hand through his hair. *Damn! The boss ain't going to be happy when he hears about this.* "Why didn't you frigging use an RPG on it? Why is it I have to do everything myself around here?"

"What? You mean you wanted us to really shoot it down? We thought the intention was to scare it off, boss," Spike said, looking confused.

"It's done now. I'm waiting on further instructions. Looks like we're about to ship out. I need you to get the truck ready. Load up and secure the hostages in the back of it. By the time you've done that, the boss should have decided what he wants us to do next. You lot get the hostages from inside. I'll deal with the bitch out here. Keep the truck hidden in the barn until the last minute, just in case the chopper returns."

The three men marched into the house through the kitchen door while Warrior traipsed across the yard again to the woman and her kid. "Time to move. Get out."

Bethany clung to her child with one arm and used the other to aid her ascent out of the hole. "Where are we going? Has my husband paid the money? Are you setting us free?"

"No, and stop asking dumb bloody questions. My threat still stands, if your other half doesn't produce that money by seven, well..." He turned the woman around and pointed at the barn off to the right. "In there."

She dragged her feet as if sensing something bad was about to happen to her. Warrior placed a hand in the middle of her back and shoved her ahead with force. "Get a move on. Stop prolonging the inevitable."

The woman hugged her crying child and began to sob. "Please, I'm willing to do anything. Just don't hurt us."

"Whatever." They entered the barn and stopped alongside the rear of the white commercial vehicle the gang had acquired, without its owner's agreement, a few months before, around the time the audacious plan had first been formulated. With one hand holding the woman's arm in case she tried to abscond again, he opened the rear of the lorry, threw back the doors then thrust the woman and the child inside. His men had prepared the lorry for this very task. They'd installed a wooden bench on either side, and bindings to hold the hostages had been placed at regular intervals along the benches. He positioned Bethany in front of the bench, took the child from her resisting arms, and placed him on the floor of the lorry. "Sit down," he ordered, securing her hands behind her back.

"But I need to hold the baby," she cried out fearfully.

"You should be more concerned about your own safety than his right now. Shut up, bitch. I'm getting tired of you always questioning what I can and can't do; you hear me?"

Her head dropped, and her chin rested on her chest. He picked up the child and left the back of the lorry. Entering the kitchen, he found the hostages all lined up, ready to ship out.

"Left holding the baby, I see." Johnny laughed.

Warrior glared at him. "Go and get the bag that he's been using as a bed. He can travel in the front, strapped in that."

Johnny rushed out of the room and returned with the bag, which he placed on the floor in front of Warrior. After tucking the baby back in his makeshift bed, Warrior walked down the line of hostages. His gaze locked, in most cases, with the terrified women and their offspring until he reached Charlie. He paused and ran his narrowed eyes the length of her young body. He jabbed a finger in her chest. "I know how that brain of yours works. If you're anything like your mother, you'll be planning your escape. I'd advise you to think again."

Charlie shrugged. "I'm not thinking anything of the sort. What do you want from us? What is this all about?"

"You've clearly missed your vocation in life, kennel maid. You should have followed in your mother's shoes, judging by the stupid questions you're asking." To ensure that he kept the other hostages in line, he slapped Charlie around the face. The other women gasped then quickly turned their heads away.

"You won't get away with this," Charlie said through gritted teeth.

"We'll see. I've already run your mother ragged today. I hope she enjoys what we have in store for her the rest of the day."

"She'll outwit you at every turn, you bastard."

"Looking for another slap, are you? Nah, I have other plans for you once we arrive at our next location, something nice and special." He turned on his heel and laughed, amused by the shock on Charlie's face. *That'll bring you down a peg or two, bitch.* His phone rang. "Load them up. I'll be with you soon."

The hostages were led out of the room, some snivelling in fear but compliant with their instructions. "Yes, boss."

"Right, here's what I've come up with at short notice. Get on the road ASAP. Your men can deal with the hostages with price tags on their heads. I have something special lined up for Simpkins's daughter."

"Rightio. What's that?"

"Never mind that for a minute. I need you to call Simpkins with these instructions…"

***

Lorne answered the phone, which had caused her to jump. "Hello."

"Good trip, I hope. Right, when you dock, I need you to jump in a taxi to complete your journey."

"Where do I take the taxi to?" Lorne asked, her anxiety levels rising as she sensed the endgame looming.

"Tell the driver to take you to the airfield at Fairoaks."

"Okay. Why? Are you flying me out of the country?"

The man applauded her assumption, and her heart sank. *Shit! I need to ring the station. Sean needs to get a team out there to help me in case I lose Tony and Joe again.*

But what Warrior had to say next floored her, ruining any such plans before they had a chance to be fully formed in her mind.

"And, Simpkins, don't even think about calling your station for help. We've already shot one chopper down. We won't hesitate to do the same to other vehicles as they approach us."

Thank God, they located the gang, but at what cost? How many lives have been lost already? "Why are you doing this? Aren't the husbands paying the ransoms?"

"Not seen a penny of the thirty mill we've ordered as yet. One thing in our favour—it would appear that taking you out of the equation was the smart option. It proves your team are useless without you."

"That's not helping the hostages or you to get the money, though, is it? I can fix this. Let me return to the station to organise the payment you need to get away. No one else needs to get hurt, please?"

"Not going to happen. Get to the airfield immediately. I have a small surprise waiting for you. I repeat, don't ring the station to give your mates an update. If you do, you can say goodbye to your little rescue centre and its occupants."

CHAPTER NINETEEN

"Hi, Katy. Bloody hell. Thought we'd lost contact for good then."

"*Sean!* Thank God. What happened?"

"One of the shots must have hit its target and knocked out our communication system, if only for a few minutes. Right, I'm here now. What's the reinforcement's status?"

"They're on their way."

"Good, I hope they're coming in force. These guys mean bloody business."

"I enforced that urgency upon the commanding officer. He said they intend hitting the place with two teams; that should cover it. Where are you now?"

"We're going to hang around out here, Katy. View things from a distance from now on. The trouble is that I have no idea what's going on at the farm. They could be up to all sorts in their blind panic, including killing the hostages."

"Crap, don't say that. They wouldn't do that surely; that would be illogical. While they have the hostages, they'll still be able to call the shots."

"Yeah, but then once their plans go awry, you know as well as I do, panic can lead these types to be unpredictable."

"Good job Lorne is out of contact with us at the moment. If she knew they had Charlie, there would be hell to pay."

"Let's keep it that way. Any news from Tony as regards to his whereabouts?"

"He called in a few minutes ago. He's located Joe and Lorne. They're on a boat cruising the river at present."

"What's that all about? These guys certainly get off on taking the piss, don't they?"

"At least we know she's safe again. My assumption is that what has occurred at the farm will probably put an end to this Warrior's futile cat-and-mouse game now."

"You're probably right. Keep me informed as and when you receive any info. We'll keep an eye open for the ARTs here."

Sean disconnected the call and instructed the pilot to circle the farm again, with caution.

***

Lorne searched the immediate area for a taxi rank. *There has to be one around here, surely!*

Relieved when a silver Mercedes taxi pulled up, she ran to the front of the queue and flashed her warrant card. "Sorry, it's a police emergency."

The disgruntled man helped his bemused wife out of the backseat of the car and objected under his breath.

Lorne gave the couple another apologetic smile then hopped in the back of the car. "Fairoaks Airfield. I need you to put your foot down; I'm on a mission."

"Right you are, love. Never been asked to do anything like this before," the driver in his thirties replied in a strong cockney accent.

Lorne couldn't help but smile at his response. If people's lives hadn't been at stake, she would probably have enjoyed the day's adventures. As it was, she was getting tired and frustrated about being a pawn in Warrior's ludicrous game. She glanced out of the window as the car sped away; Tony was standing on the kerb, thumping his fist against his good leg. With no other taxis in sight, she realised the chances of him keeping up with her were minimal. She was on her own again. *I'm sorry, darling. It looks like this one is down to me from now on.*

***

Warrior watched the last of the hostages being loaded into the back of the lorry. He had a firm grip on Charlie. Her look of disgust and open desire to throttle him didn't go unnoticed, either. "Why? Let them go. At the end of the day, isn't this really about me and my mother?"

He had to admire the girl's guts and astuteness. "Shut up. It's not *all* about you. Well, in a way it is, but ultimately, there's thirty mill of goods sitting in there. You're an added bonus if you like." Charlie raised her leg and stamped on his foot. Warrior tightened his grip with one hand and slapped her around the face with the other. "Feisty little *shit*, ain't you?"

"I have my moments. I'm not scared of you guys. I've been in tighter fixes than this and come out of them unscathed. I can tell what a crap setup this is. You haven't got a clue what you're doing. Your men couldn't even take the police helicopter down. And talking of the police, you really think they won't attack this place with armed men soon? Are you nuts? Or just plain stupid?"

"You'll get what's coming to you, bitch. For now, I'm under strict orders not to hurt you, but the boss said I could do what I like to you once you've been delivered to your final destination. I might even let the other guys take their turn with you, too, as punishment for being so lippy."

Charlie tilted her head back and laughed. "You think that threat is going to scare me?" She looked inside the lorry at the terrified faces of the women and children tied to their seats. One by one, the women turned away. It didn't concern Charlie; she'd been in the same situation before and had grown in stature since her time under the Unicorn's confinement. Her willpower and survival instincts would see her through the ordeal; she was confident about that.

Warrior leaned towards her and shouted in her ear, "It should *effing* worry you, girl. If you thought the Unicorn was bad, he was an absolute pussycat to my men. You'd be well advised to shut up and just enjoy the ride for now, because we have a different form of ride in store for you later." He laughed, and so did the men around them.

Charlie looked at him, her eyes narrowing in anger. "Words are cheap," she taunted.

The remark earned her another slap before Warrior ordered her to get in the vehicle. Sneering, Johnny tied her roughly then ran his hands down her neck and over her breasts. He tweaked her nipple. Charlie refused to cry out in pain. She needed to keep up the pretence that the men didn't frighten her. Displaying some of her mother's spirit was the only way she was going to get out of the scenario alive. *I'll make you proud of me, Mum.* Once all the hostages were restrained, the men locked the back of the lorry. In the darkness, the children began to scream and cry out for their mothers. As her eyes adjusted to the darkness, Charlie asked, "Is everyone all right?"

One voice replied, "Yes, barely. No thanks to you."

"I've been in a similar situation before. I assure you being carefree and feisty is the only way for us to survive this."

The woman who had spoken before snorted. "I think you're wrong, young lady. Your foolishness is likely to get you, and *us*, killed in the process. Now shut up. Don't try and drag us into your ridiculously naive plan. I think I speak for all of us. Don't I, ladies?"

"You do. I want no part of your outrageous plan," said one of the other women, then a little voice in the corner agreed.

Charlie shook her head. "Fine. That suits me. But you have my word on this, ladies. I *will* get out of this fix alive."

"We'll see," the first woman replied coarsely.

Well that was unexpected. Looks like you're on your own in this, Charlie girl! She shrugged her acceptance as the lorry pulled away.

***

Sean pointed at the lorry below. "They're leaving. Shit! Where are the reinforcements?" He rang the station, and Katy picked up.

"Where are they? The kidnappers are getting away."

"Shit! I'll get onto them ASAP. They assured me they were on their way. I'll get back to you in a mo with an update, boss."

Sean disconnected the call. "Wonder where they are heading. Damn, I didn't see the lorry back there, did you?"

The pilot shook his head. "They could be heading anywhere. I think we should still keep our distance just in case they open fire on us again."

"Agreed," Sean replied before he answered his ringing mobile. "Katy? What did they say?"

"There was some kind of hold-up with one of the teams. I again specified the urgency, and they've assured me it's all in hand and that they're on their way."

"Well, it's going to be too late. The lorry is already five minutes ahead of them. I'm not privy to their route, so have no idea where to send them. Jesus, this is a logistical nightmare."

"You're not wrong there. Can you continue to follow them?"

"We'll do our best with the fuel we have." Sean looked over at the gauges on the dashboard, and the pilot pointed at the fuel gauge. "We've got about half a tank."

"What about if we set up some kind of roadblock? Will that help?" Katy suggested.

"It might if we knew what direction they were heading in. At the moment, the lorry is still making its way down the country lanes. The main road is coming up about five miles ahead. We'll know more then. Standby, Katy. I'll call you back when we reach it."

The pilot weaved in and out and circled the lorry, keeping his movements erratic in case the gang opened fire again. Once they reached the main road, Sean called the station again. "Katy, it looks to me like the lorry is heading for the M25. Which direction it takes then, I have no idea."

"Great! They couldn't be heading for that motorway at a worse time. It's almost six, and the rush-hour traffic will be building soon. It won't be long before it lives up to its tag of being the world's largest car park."

"Yep, my thoughts exactly. If only we could figure out a way of cutting it off before the lorry reaches it."

"I hear you, boss, except going down that route could endanger the hostages' lives."

"I'm aware of that, Sergeant. I'm just fed up with sitting back and letting this gang walk all over us. Aren't you?"

"Of course I am. There's no point us falling out about this. What do you want me to do at this end? If I were running the show, I'd hold off trying to intercept the lorry. Gather all the relative teams and form a convoy, ready to set up a rescue attempt once the vehicle has come to a standstill."

"Okay, we'll do things your way. Notify all the teams, including the ARTs, to remain on standby and give them our location, Katy. I'll be in touch soon."

CHAPTER TWENTY

Lorne surveyed the view of the passing countryside, thankful that she didn't have a chatty driver bombarding her with inane conversation. She felt strangely relaxed in spite of the stress she'd dealt with for most of the day. Every now and again, she took a hopeful glance out of the back window to see if there was any sign of Tony. There wasn't. She drummed her fingers on her knees and wondered what lay ahead of her. The squeal of tyres tightened her stomach, and she prepared herself for the impact.

Once the white van hit the side of the car, the taxi driver shot out of the vehicle, and with his fists raised, he threatened the other driver. Lorne jumped out of the car and inserted herself in between the angry men. "Stop it. Accidents happen."

"Nice touch, lady. Not to my bloody taxi, it doesn't. It's frigging new! I've only had it a week. Look at it—it's a write-off!"

Lorne cringed when she turned to examine the damage. "Hardly, but it's not in good nick, granted. Look, I'm sorry to rush you, but I need to get to the airfield."

The driver curled his lip and looked at her with contempt. "Are you effing kidding me? How do you propose I take you? In that?"

"Well, yes."

The driver shook his head and mumbled under his breath as he walked back to the driver's door. "Stupid woman hasn't got a bloody clue!"

Lorne didn't know whether to laugh openly at the man's chuntering or slap the cuffs on him for insulting a police officer.

The driver returned, holding a pen and paper in his hand. "I want your name and address."

Lorne pointed at her chest. "Mine? Why?"

"You're a witness to the accident, a valuable one at that, given what you do for a living."

"Before I do that, I want to know if you've requested a replacement cab?"

"Yep, it's all in hand. The other driver should be here within fifteen minutes."

Lorne flung her arms out to the side. "What? Nothing sooner?"

"Nope, take it or leave it, lady. Make up your mind quick if you want to leave it, and I'll get onto the control room again."

She shrugged. "Doesn't look like I have a lot of choice, does it?"

"That's right." He held his pad up and stepped in front of the other driver. "Come on, hand 'em over. I want your name and address and insurance details."

"Ah," the driver of the white van said, "I haven't got insurance. I was going to pay for it this weekend when my wages have come through."

"Shit! So you're uninsured and someone has let you loose on the road without you knowing your highway code. Is that it? Christ, this day just keeps getting better and better."

Think yourself lucky, mate! You should see what my day has involved thus far.

Out of the blue, the van driver whacked the taxi driver in the jaw, knocking him to the ground.

Lorne cursed under her breath and dipped her hand in her pocket to retrieve her cuffs. "Not a smart move, buster. You're under arrest," she told the van driver.

"Shit! You're a bloody copper? What for?"

"Assault."

He held up his hands in resignation. Lorne looked around to find somewhere she could secure the man to until uniformed officers arrived. In the end, she hooked one end of the cuffs to the steering wheel of the van and the other one around his wrist. By then, the taxi driver was beginning to stir.

He glanced up at her and rubbed his jaw. "I hope you've arrested him?"

"I have. Let's just all remain calm until help arrives, eh?" Lorne pleaded.

"Have you rung the station?"

"Not yet. Do you have a mobile I can use?"

Puzzled, he said, "Are you telling me you don't carry a phone with you?"

"It's a long story, one that I'd rather not go into if you don't mind." Lorne held out her hand for his phone. He slapped it into her open palm and muttered something incomprehensible. Her mind went blank as she struggled to remember the number of the station; otherwise, she would have called Katy. Instead, she dialled 999. "Police please, there's been an accident." She gave the woman on control her location and a brief outline of what had occurred.

"I see, ma'am. We'll get a car out there ASAP."

"Great. Emphasise the need for urgency, if you will. As soon as another cab arrives, I need to leave the scene immediately."

"I understand, ma'am."

She spent the next ten minutes warding off scowls from both men until finally a patrol car arrived to take care of the two men. Not long after that, a replacement taxi turned up. The new driver tried to get into a conversation with the other taxi driver, but Lorne flashed her warrant card and asked him to get on the road right away.

The driver tried to squeeze information out of her about how the accident had happened, but Lorne remained quiet, silently begging him to hush. She regretted not continuing her journey with the other driver.

"How long will it take us to get there?"

"It depends on the traffic. Rush hour is upon us. Between thirty and forty minutes. In a hurry are you?"

"Yes, you could say that."

"Maybe you should carry one of those police blue lights in your pocket." He laughed at his own joke, but ceased quickly when Lorne grunted her annoyance at the quip.

Yep, it's going to be a long journey now!

***

"Hi, Katy. It's Tony. We've lost Lorne. She gave us the slip, I'm guessing under instructions, at the pier."

"Damn. That's not good news, Tony. Things are accelerating pretty damn quickly."

"Shit! In what way?"

"The gang are on the move. Sean's tailing them for now, but his pilot is being forced to use more fuel to try and dodge another attack."

"Right. Well, rather than staying out here, twiddling our bloody thumbs, you tell us what to do. Where do you want us? It's your call, Katy."

"I don't know what to suggest. We're all in limbo until we know what's going on with the lorry. I have two ARTs trying to track it down, plus Sean up in the chopper. Seriously, I think it would be best if you try and locate Lorne yourself."

"How the heck are we supposed to do that, Katy?"

"I know; it was a stupid comment. She's out there, cut off from us. It sucks big time."

"You're not wrong. I have an idea. Let me make a call, and I'll get back to you."

Tony disconnected the call and immediately dialled another number.

"Who are you ringing?" Joe asked.

He winked at his partner and held up a finger, telling him to wait a moment. "Hi, Carol. How are you feeling now?"

Joe tutted and shook his head. He was a total sceptic.

"A lot better now my head has stopped spinning. Any news, love?"

"First of all, we know where Charlie is. We believe she's with the other hostages."

Carol gasped. "Oh my, that's not good news."

"I'd rather be inclined to disagree with you there, Carol. The likelihood of the hostages being hurt is minimal, I'd say. I could be talking nonsense, of course—we have no way of telling how it will pan out once the kidnappers have got their hands on the ransom money they're demanding."

"Okay, what about Lorne? Is she safe?"

"That's really why I'm ringing you. We've lost contact with her. It was an intentional strategy from the kidnappers. I hate to ask this when you're feeling so fragile, and I'm aware how much energy channelling your spirits takes out of you, but we're desperate, Carol. Can you see if you can give us some form of clue where to look next?"

Carol fell quiet for a moment. "I see a long, long stretch of road. No traffic, just tarmac."

"Okay, I guess that rules out the M25 then."

"There's really no need for you to worry about her. She's in safe hands."

"At this exact moment maybe. She got a ride in a cab. Who knows where that cab will lead her and who'll be awaiting her arrival at the other end?"

"That's not what I'm picking up, Tony. Hush a second…"

Tony tapped his foot on the pavement and swayed gently back and forth as if Carol's om mantra were putting him under a spell. Joe clicked his fingers in front of Tony's face. Tony snapped out of his trance and held the phone away from his ear until Carol spoke aloud.

"Don't laugh when I say this—you know how this works. Pete is watching over her; he'll ensure nothing bad happens to her. I have no ill-feelings about this. Yes, she's in danger, but he'll ring her with a shield of protection. Sam is there in the background, too. However, Pete is the one who has been handed the task to watch over her from above."

"That's all very reassuring, Carol. I appreciate what you're saying. Now, can you home in on a location? This road, does it lead to a deserted warehouse perhaps? Is that why it's empty?"

"It's all rather fuzzy still—my head, not the visions. Let me try and focus more." After a brief pause, she added, "There is some kind of huge building. I can roughly see the outline. Perhaps it is a warehouse after all. I'm sorry I can't add more, Tony. I truly am."

"You've done really well, considering you're recovering from a bump on the head. We'll find her. I'll start searching the map now for possible locations. I take it this road is still in this area, the London area?"

"It's hard to say. I think so."

"Thanks, Carol. I'll keep you informed."

"Please do. I'm praying that Charlie and Lorne remain safe and that their feistiness doesn't land them in hot water."

"I'm hoping that too."

Tony ended the call and peered over Joe's shoulder. His partner had already pulled up Google Earth on his mobile.

"The problem is the size of area we're dealing with," Joe said.

"I know. It's all we have to go on, mate. A long straight road..."

Joe looked at him, and in sync, their eyes widened. They both shouted, "A runway!"

Tony rang Katy again. "Katy, we have an idea where Lorne might be heading. I just rang Carol, and she told us that Lorne would end up on a long stretch of road with nothing on it. There would also be a huge building in sight. Well, I immediately thought of some kind of disused warehouse, but now Joe and I think we should be looking for a runway."

"Wow! Really. Shit! You think they're going to get her on a plane and transfer her out of the country?"

"Well, I hadn't really thought that far ahead, but now you've mentioned it, yes, that's a succinct possibility."

"What about the hostages? Did Carol pick up anything about them? Will they be harmed in any way? Furthermore, what about Charlie?"

"Honestly, I don't know. All Carol picked up was that Lorne, although she's in danger, Pete is protecting her. We need you to help us find this runway or airfield, Katy. I doubt that we're looking at one of the major airports in or around London."

"How do you know that, Tony?"

"I don't really, I'm speculating more than anything. Too much security, for a start. They'll want to keep her out of the public eye. I would, if I were in their shoes, knowing her reputation."

"You're right. So AJ and I will look for a smaller airfield that takes private planes. How's that?"

"Perfect. Can you perhaps look at a thirty-mile radius of the centre of London? It needs to be fairly accessible for the kidnappers, I would have thought."

"Let me see what we can find and get back to you."

"We'll search for some kind of transport in the interim." Tony watched Joe walk away and approach two men. He pulled out a wad of notes and returned wearing a broad smile and carrying two motorcycle helmets. "Money talks, eh?"

Joe nodded. "What better form of transport than those beauties." He nodded at the pristine Kawasaki motorcycles.

"Jesus, I haven't ridden one of those since I was a spook! Not sure how the leg will hold up."

"Nonsense. You'll be fine. I told the guys we were MI6 agents in a covert operation and promised to take care of them."

"Stretching the truth a little there, mate," Tony said as they crossed the road to collect the vehicles.

The men seemed anxious but handed over the keys anyway. Tony and Joe climbed on their respective bikes, revved the engines then set off.

CHAPTER TWENTY-ONE

The taxi arrived at the airfield. "Drop you at the entrance, shall I, love?"

"I presume so. I'm meeting someone." She paid the driver and watched from the pavement as he sped off. She wasn't alone for long, though. Another car pulled up alongside her, and the passenger door was flung open. She bent down, and her heart almost stopped when she saw the man who'd been issued with the task of following her behind the steering wheel, glaring at her. "Get in."

Lorne straightened and quickly searched around her in the hope that someone might come to her rescue before she got in the car. However, the road was empty. Reluctantly, she dropped into the passenger seat. "Where are you taking me?"

"You'll find out soon enough."

The car drove into the next road and entered the airfield through some kind of tradesman's entrance. Lorne eyed the driver with concern as he went past a hangar; a private jet loomed ahead of them. *Shit! They're going to take me out of the country. Pete, if you're around, please help me before it's too late.* Lorne shuddered when a slight breeze brushed her neck; she swiftly turned in her seat to find it empty. Upon closer inspection, she found a used Kit Kat wrapper poking out from a crease in the back of the seat. She turned to face the plane again and found that her anxiety level had dropped a little.

The car stopped at the bottom of the plane's steps. The driver left the car and opened the passenger door. "Get out."

"I see you're a man of many words," Lorne mumbled, grinning at him.

His eyes narrowed. He grabbed her elbow and pulled her up the steps and into the cabin of the plane. Lorne's heart raced when she entered the cabin and saw a smartly dressed man smoking a huge Havana cigar, awaiting her arrival.

"Well, well, well, I finally get to meet the intrepid Lorne Simpkins."

She noted the man spoke with an Eastern European accent. He exhaled a vast plume of smoke, which drifted swiftly through the cabin and into her face.

She wafted the smoke away with her hand. "That'll be Lorne Warner. Do I know you?"

"We've never met. However, I know all I need to know about you, Detective Inspector. The question is what I do with you now that I have you in my *possession.*"

The way he emphasised the word *possession* made her skin prickle in fear. She was determined to remain blasé about her situation and not to let the man know how scared she was of being in his company. She would do her utmost to live up to the reputation he'd already attributed to her.

The driver left the plane, and she heard the car pull away. "What are your intentions? And how am I connected to the hostages you have abducted in the past few days? Apart from being the investigating officer, that is."

"Questions, questions. All will be revealed soon enough. Take a seat." He pointed to a plush leather swivel chair close to him.

"No. I'd rather stand."

"Come now, Inspector. After the traumatic day you've had, I would've thought your weary legs would be screaming for a rest by now." His laughter rebounded off the cabin walls.

"I'll sit once you've told me what you want?"

He shrugged and inhaled another drag of his cigar. Once he'd exhaled another large swell of smoke, he replied, "It's simple really—I want *you*."

"Well, you can't have me. I'm married. Did I mention my husband is an MI6 agent?" She tried to bluff her way out of the intense situation.

He laughed again then fixed her with a glare. "Don't mess with me, Simpkins. He's an *ex*-MI6 agent with a dodgy leg. Don't expect him to come to your rescue, either. My men have already dealt with him and his agent buddy who were tailing you, not as covertly as it happens. They've been more like a couple of keystone cops than highly trained agents during today's exercise. The little adventure conducted during the course of the day has been a test, for all of you. I needed to know each of your limits and capabilities. I've well and truly accomplished that now."

"And what have you deduced?" Lorne challenged him.

"That, my dear lady, is for me to know. Let's just say with regard to you, I was not surprised by my findings."

"So what happens now?" Lorne asked.

"You owe me, Simpkins, and I'm about to get my compensation and some."

***

Katy tapped her foot impatiently. "Answer the damn phone, Tony."

Finally, her call was answered. "Katy, hi. Sorry, we were in transit."

"Where to? I've been calling you for ages."

"It doesn't matter. Do you have an inkling about which airfield we should be heading for?"

"After careful consideration, AJ and I both think you should try Fairoaks. It seems the most plausible to us."

"I think I know it. I'll pull up the directions on the phone. Look, Joe and I have acquired a pair of Kawasaki motorbikes, so we should reach there quicker than we normally would. What if we're wrong?"

"Don't worry. I'm sending teams out to the other airfields in the area just in case. If I hear back from any of them with a sighting, I'll let you know."

"Fair enough."

"Tony, bring her home. We need her."

"Roger that, Katy."

Katy ended the call and fell into the chair next to her. AJ threw an arm around her shoulder and kissed her forehead lightly. "Stick with it, Katy. You're doing a fabulous job."

"I'm exhausted, AJ. Lord knows how Lorne must be feeling."

"She'll push herself through the exhaustion. She's resilient; you know that."

"Then, if she can do it, so can I. Have we heard from Sean lately?"

She picked up the phone and dialled AJ's mobile when her partner shook his head. "Sean? What's going on?"

"I was just about to ring you. We were in a dip; bad communication area. Things are certainly heating up, Katy. The four-by-four is now in use, and they transferred one of the hostages into it."

"Did you see who it was, Sean?"

"No. However, an educated guess is telling me it might have been Charlie. Then the vehicles split off in different directions. I decided it would be best to keep the lorry in our sight. It was a tough decision to make, Katy."

"Damn! Okay, we need to try and put a halt to this, boss. I'm inclined to go with a roadblock now. What do you think?"

"Yep, I agree. Action it ASAP. The lorry is approaching junction 26 on the M25. Maybe they'll be heading for the channel tunnel. It's a guess, but we should stop it before it goes much farther."

"I'm on it. Be in touch soon."

Katy actioned the Armed Response Team to ambush the lorry. The commanding officer said that they were prepared and would instigate the plan immediately.

Katy hung up and blew out a relieved breath. She winced as Charlie's face drifted into her mind. She crossed her fingers and closed her eyes to say a silent prayer for the girl's safety.

CHAPTER TWENTY-TWO

The helicopter kept the lorry within sight. Sean surveyed the surrounding area, on the lookout for the ARTs. At least this part of the motorway appeared to be light of traffic, further inspection over his shoulder showed a queue of traffic being held up by a police roadblock, which was a blessing. Sean angled the binoculars ahead. He saw two large parked vehicles, one on either side of the motorway, and around ten cars in front of the lorry. As the final car passed, something was dispatched across the surface of the motorway by a man. Glinting in the sun's rays as it landed, the object caught Sean's eye. He realised the teams had placed a Stinger across the three lanes. As the driver applied the brakes, smoke clouds erupted from its tyres. The vehicle swerved violently and ended up sidelong across the motorway as it tried to avoid the Stinger, but it was too late.

Sean punched the air, and the pilot winked at him and issued a satisfied smile. Once the lorry ground to a halt, two armed men left the cabin and aimed their rifles at the ART vehicles. Sean noticed another chopper had joined them and pointed it out to the pilot. "Doesn't take long for Sky News to get in on the action, eh?"

The pilot shrugged and exhaled an annoyed breath. "They better keep out of my way. Do you want me to land? We'll probably be safer down there than up here, by the looks of things."

"Yes, take her down. The news crew might get the hint and withdraw from the area."

Sean watched as a shootout began between the ART and the kidnappers. One of the kidnappers hit the tarmac, screaming in agony and holding his right thigh. The other kidnapper had seen enough; he threw aside his weapon and held up his hands in surrender. Sean punched the air for a second time and rang the station as the helicopter landed.

"Katy, we've got them. I repeat—the hostages are safe."

"That's fantastic news. I'll ring Tony, let him know."

"You do that. I'm just going to sort things out here, and then I'll get up in the air, see if we can track down the four-by-four."

"Okay, Tony and Joe are on their way to Fairoaks Airfield. We think that's where Lorne is located."

"Interesting. That's a fair distance from here. What if the four-by-four is on its way there to meet up with Lorne?"

"Maybe. How long has it been since you last laid eyes on it?"

"Around twenty minutes, tops. Let me check the hostages, and make sure it was Charlie they unloaded from the lorry. I'll call you back."

Sean raced across the motorway, showed his ID, and went to the back of the lorry, which had been opened by a couple of ART members. He scanned the terrified faces looking his way and shook his head. "Did they separate Charlie?"

"Yes." A woman cradling her infant nodded. "I hope they don't harm her."

"So do I," Sean replied, turning and racing back to the chopper.

He contacted the station again to tell Katy that his assumption was spot on, then he instructed the pilot to head for the airfield Katy had suggested the kidnappers might be using to hold Lorne.

***

Lorne stared at the unknown man, trying to match the glare he was aiming at her. Every now and again, when he closed his eyes to take another satisfying drag on his cigar, Lorne's eyes flitted around the cabin, looking for something she could use as a weapon, or to plan her escape. She saw only two doors in the cabin: one she presumed led to the cockpit and the one where she'd entered the plane. The second was still open, ensuring a steady flow of fresh air circulated the cabin.

She inhaled a large breath and smiled. "Are you going to tell me how you know of me?"

"A mutual acquaintance, shall we say." His laughter was filled with provocation.

"You need to give me more than that if we're going to go forward and work with each other."

"Who said anything about working *with* each other?" His eyes narrowed to tiny slits.

Lorne pinched her temple with her finger and thumb as the beginning of a headache emerged. "Then what are you expecting from me?"

"I expect you to pay me back. It's taken me almost seven years to be in a position to track you down."

"You're still not making any sense. I'm hearing what you're saying, but I'm struggling to formulate an idea as to what you are getting at."

His gaze left hers while he stubbed out the cigar in a large glass ashtray. Lorne seized her opportunity and lunged for the open door. He was on her in a flash—he grabbed her wrist, and before she could take a step out of the plane, he yanked her back inside the cabin.

"Let go of me, you brute." Her legs and arms lashed out as much as they could, but with him sitting upright on her chest, her efforts proved to be hopeless.

All of a sudden, his face turned serious. He leaned forward and grasped both of her wrists, pinning them on either side of her head. Lorne squeezed her eyes tightly shut, fearing that his mouth was about to cover hers. Another person spoke in the cabin, forcing her eyes open again. She recognised the voice of the man standing at the cockpit door as Warrior. The man sitting on top of her growled at him, "Get back in there and leave this bitch to me. I have such illicit plans for her before…"

Before what, shithead? My demise? "Get off me!" Lorne shouted. She lifted her legs, trying to knee the man in the back to dislodge him. Her attempt was shafted, not by the brute thwarting her efforts, but by a female voice.

"Mum! Mum, is that you?"

Her eyes widened. *"Charlie!* Oh my God, what are you doing here, darling? Have they hurt you? Do as they say." *For now*, she added in her mind.

"I'm all right, Mum," Charlie cried out.

The man slapped Lorne hard around the face, instantly sapping the breath from her body. He turned to shout at Warrior, "Get back in there. Take the girl with you while I deal with her mother. Silence her any way you see fit." He laughed, raising his head backwards and imitating a wolf calling for its mate in the wild. "They'll have to get used to what we have in store for them. It's how they'll be working off the debt they owe me from now on."

Lorne shook her head. "I owe you nothing. I don't even know you, for fuck's sake."

He slapped her again, twice, with the back and the palm of his hand, then stood up, dragging her to her feet by her hair as the cockpit door slammed shut. She couldn't help straining her ear in the direction of the cockpit, more concerned with her daughter's safety than her own. However, she was greeted with silence. She prayed that Charlie would behave herself in there with Warrior and not prompt him into punishing her.

As the man yanked her to her feet again, Lorne caught a glimpse of daylight through the door. She hoped to see some form of backup gathering to rescue her, but found nothing of the kind. The man threw her into the chair again. Something smashed against her leg, and she shifted her position, trying not to give away what had happened under the man's intensive gaze. Suddenly, the object in her pocket gave her strength to tackle him, if only verbally for the time being.

"At least give me your name."

"It's Alexei Popovski."

"I don't recognise the name. What harm would it do to fill me in on who you are? I promise, I won't try to run again."

"And your word has always been your bond. Hasn't it, Simpkins?"

She ground her teeth at the way he twisted her old name around his evil tongue. She shrugged. "Again, I have no idea what you're implying. Why don't you lay all of your cards on the table? Go on—at least have the guts to do that."

He reached into the engraved wooden box next to him and removed another cigar. He took his time preparing to light it, adding to her frustration. She forced herself to remain patient; he was clearly revelling in his ability to have some kind of hold over her. Lorne wriggled in her seat, freeing the object in her pocket, making it accessible to her if she made another attempt to escape. The only problem with that was she had Charlie's safety to consider as well as her own. *Dilemma, dilemma. This day has been filled with bloody dilemmas, none as large as this, though.*

They heard Charlie shout. Her daughter's raised voice seemed to amuse Popovski.

Lorne glared at him and ordered, "Let her go. Do what you want to me, but please let her go. She doesn't belong here."

"Oh, you're so wrong about that, Inspector. She actually belongs to me, has done for a very long time."

Lorne's brain began to function properly again and recounted the scenario she had come up with at the start of the kidnapping case. "Are you telling me that you are linked to the Unicorn?"

He placed his cigar in his mouth and clapped slowly. "Bravo, Inspector. I knew you would succeed in finding the answers if I left you to work it out long enough. Along with that success should come the realisation to your assumption. I own *both* you and your daughter. Especially your *daughter*. She was on my payroll at one point. Am I wrong?"

Lorne's lip curled up. She was tempted to fly at him and rip the cold black eyes from his head. "My daughter has never, nor will ever, belong to anyone. She's a British citizen and lives in a free world."

"You're wrong." He pointed to his chest. "I *own* her. I was in partnership with Baldwin. We'll dispense of the stupid name he preferred to call himself. She was put to work at one of our more salubrious locations, or so I was told. It was unfortunate that Baldwin took her virginity from her. I could have sold her for far more when the time was right. That man foolishly only thought with his dick at times. He was never quite able to grasp the idea that virgins commanded a higher figure on the open market. He was such a greedy man. I know of a way I can make her a virgin once again. It involves a small surgical procedure, but it will be worth it in the end." He rubbed his hands together in glee before the cockpit flew open again. "What do you want now?"

"Boss, we've got company. A helicopter has just landed."

"We're at an airfield, man. What do you expect?"

"This is different, boss. There were two men waiting for the passenger when he left the chopper. They have bikes. I don't like the look of it, and I'd suggest that we take to the sky sooner rather than later."

"Very well. Get the pilot to prepare for take-off. Strap the girl in a seat up front with you, and I'll make the inspector comfy back here with me."

"Yes, boss. I'll shut the door."

Lorne strained her neck, trying to see out of one of the small windows, but it was impossible. Her heart raced at the thought of help arriving soon and of Tony being close by, if in fact it was him they were referring to. He would have to action a rescue attempt quickly, though. She had to figure out a way of stalling the plane from taking off.

The plane's engines roared to life, and as Warrior swept past them to hoist up the steps and close the door, Lorne dipped her hand into her pocket. She withdrew the pepper spray and aimed it in his face before she turned the can on Popovski, who'd taken pleasure in taunting her. She managed to stall the two men long enough for her to get to the door of the plane and scream for assistance.

"Help! I'm being abducted! Help me." At the perimeter fence, she could make out two men on bikes and another man talking to them. All three men looked in her direction. That was all she saw before Popovski yanked her back and shoved her into her seat once more. This time, it wasn't his open hand that connected with her jaw—it was his clenched fist. For a second, everything took place in slow motion.

The plane began to move. Lorne struggled to remain focused, but when a man wearing a helmet jumped aboard the plane, it jolted her mind to focus on the unfolding events. The plane began to swerve as the three men fought. Lorne was eager to jump in and help her rescuer, but within seconds of his timely arrival, he had the situation under control. Her two abductors were soon lying unconscious on the floor, and the plane's tyres screeched as the pilot applied the brakes.

"Quick, Charlie is in the cockpit. I have no idea how many more men are in there."

"It's all right, Lorne. I'll get her," the man assured her, his voice muffled by the helmet.

Recognising the voice, she smiled and whispered, "Thanks, Joe." He gave her a gun and told her to stand over the two men in case they woke up. The plane shuddered to a halt. Sean and Tony rushed up the steps and boarded the plane. Sean took the gun from her hand while Tony enfolded her in his arms. "Oh, Tony, I thought I'd lost you. He said he'd dealt with you. I thought he'd killed…"

"Well, he didn't. The Taliban couldn't kill me, and neither could this idiot. You're stuck with me for life, Lorne Warner."

He kissed her, a long deep kiss that reflected the magnitude of their love. Once they released each other, Lorne turned to her left to find an amused-looking Sean shaking his head at them. "When you two have quite finished."

Charlie came out of the cockpit, sprinting like a champion greyhound. Lorne held her tightly, tears spilling from her eyes as she planted dozens of kisses over Charlie's face. "Darling, we're safe. I love you so much."

"I love you too, Mum. What would have happened to us if we hadn't been rescued? They were linked to the Unicorn, weren't they?"

"It would appear so, love, yes. It's best not to think about that now." She swept a hand over her beautiful daughter's face.

"Will this kind of thing crop up in the future, Mum? Will more of his associates try to get their own back on us?"

Lorne glanced at Sean then at Tony. Charlie had a valid point. Who knew what sadistic creatures roamed the earth on the lookout for revenge because of Lorne's success at spoiling their heinous plots of world domination. Life would continue to be full of unwanted surprises going forward—of that, Lorne had no doubt. It would be up to her and her team to continue to rid the world of such evil wrongdoers.

THE END

Note to the reader.

Thank you for reading CALCULATED JUSTICE; I sincerely hope you enjoyed reading this novel as much as I loved writing it.

If you liked it, please consider posting a short review as genuine feedback is what makes all the lonely hours writers spend producing their work worthwhile.

Never miss a new release, sign up to M A Comley's newsletter now. Subscribe to newsletter

Made in the USA
Charleston, SC
19 August 2015